Hi mom

Holey Buy Bull

by

DJAss Maggots

Cover Illustrations and design by Krayola

This book is dedicated to my good friend and colleague
Ilyas Somer Karaalp (May 6, 1967–July 14, 2017)

We all work too hard to appreciate the fragility of life.

This book is also dedicated to my cousin
Amirali Zandpour (June 10, 1981–February 18, 2017)
A gentle guy, taken too soon back to the stars . . .
"Check it out, cuz. i wrote another crazy book!"

Like a caterpillar to a butterfly,
Ass Maggots to a shart.

Contents

More Alone Than Alone

Hey, man, where'd you go? i had to return your car to the dealership, and everyone on Lakewood Boulevard was looking at me like they'd seen a ghost. Remember when we used to race down Lakewood Boulevard toward the traffic circle— you in your BMW M4 convertible, gray with red interior, me in my white Lamborghini Murcielago Roadster? i should have won every race, man. My car was faster, and i was a crazier driver, willing to take risks, go on the wrong side of the road to beat you. But you were the reliable one. You just stayed in your lane, accelerating as much as that precise German engineering would allow. Me? i was all over the place. Those Italian cars . . . my tires would blow, my engine would smoke, cops would pull me over. And so you won half the races. Because you were the reliable one. You were always the reliable one . . .

AND WHERE THE FUCK ARE YOU NOW!!!!!!!?????

Where the fuck are you now? You were the reliable one. i tried to go to Sweden for a week . . . and i know . . . work was crazy . . . patients were dying left and right. Summer's supposed to be the slow season in the hospital. But things were really busy. And something was going on with your blood pressure or something. Why didn't you get it checked? Why didn't you get a stress test, with your family history and all? Why didn't you have life insurance? Why didn't you have estate planning? Now my sister has to find one of her probate attorney friends to figure all this shit out. Could take a year. Now i'm the reliable one, going through your home office paperwork with your wife, biller, and accountant. *i'm* the reliable one. And you're dead. Shhhhh . . . baby, shhhhhh . . . baby. Baby, don't cry. Baby, don't cry.

You know those five stages of grief? i got stuck on the anger stage for a while, man. Well, your wife and your daughters are watching this now. The guy i had lunch with almost every day for the last ten years is gone. And so i tell your wife that i feel alone. And she looks at me like, "You feel alone? I've lost my husband. My daughters have lost their father." She's right. She must be like ten times more alone than me, maybe a hundred. What's ten times zero? Still zero. In math class they taught us that anything times zero is zero. But are all zeros equal? A person can't be more alone than alone? Math sucks.

Remember how you would watch my open mics and tell me they're pretty good, but i gotta lose the papers? They're distracting. i should memorize this stuff. Well, surprise, surprise. i memorized this one. This paper? This is your actual death certificate. i signed it myself. Remember how we would kind of joke and say you could tell how busy the hospital was by how many death certificates we signed a week? Sometimes one a day. Well, this is yours. Remember how you'd ask me for advice on what to put on the diagnosis line on the complicated ones? And i'd say, "Man, forget about all that stuff. The mortuary wants us to keep it simple. Just put 'cardiopulmonary arrest for minutes, coronary artery disease for years.' For most adults, that's pretty much the standard line." Well, that's how i filled out yours: cardiopulmonary arrest for minutes, coronary artery disease for years.

Look, dude, i'm not trying to get depressing. This isn't the end. It's the beginning of a new line of communication. So make sure you got a good Wi-Fi connection up there. And i assume the G.O.D. would have 4G LTE coverage. So we'll talk again next week. i gotta go. i just messed up the ambiance for a young comedian who's just trying to make some nice folks laugh. i'm out. Peace, brother.

—for Dr. Ilyas Somer Karaalp

May 6, 1967–July 14, 2017

(performed live onstage)

i Got Ninety-Nine Problems, and This Lamborghini Is All of 'Em

Lamborghini Service Advisor 1: "We're gonna have to replace your E-gear for six thousand dollars, and your engine is five quarts low on oil. And we'll be taking the engine out for the E-gear, so in case you need a new engine, that will be fifty-five thousand dollars."

Me: "What? Why would i need a new engine?"

Lamborghini Service Advisor 1: "I don't think you will need one. Just letting you know since the engine is coming out."

A few weeks later . . .

Lamborghini Service Advisor 2: "We did that oil-leak test that you authorized for seven hundred dollars and did not find anything. So the next step is a new engine, which will cost a hundred twenty thousand dollars."

Me: "Wait, what? Who are you? What happened to the last guy?"

Lamborghini Service Advisor 2: "He was promoted. And this is my first week working at Lamborghini."

Me: "i've never heard of a new engine as the second step for oil loss in a car with only thirteen thousand miles. Just put in the E-gear, and i'll come pick my car up."

A month later . . .

Lamborghini Service Advisor 3: "Good news—your new engine is in, and your car should be good to go by tomorrow."

Me: "WHAT?! i absolutely did NOT authorize a new engine. And what happened to the last guy?"

Lamborghini Service Advisor 3: "He was terminated. Ummm, let me check on your car and get back to you."

So . . . i was able to retrieve the car, without a new engine. i think it's time to leave the Italian car world and buy a Tesla.

i Need Someone to Gift Me a Free Ticket to Burning Man, Stat!

i also need a ride up there. And a place to stay. And food and water. i can totally pay for gas, as long as we go to a gas station that accepts EBT. Not that i use EBT, it's just that those gas stations usually have ATM machines where my credit card will work—it has a crack in it.

If you provide me food, it must be vegan (chicken and fish are OK), gluten-free (i have nouveau tropical sprue), non-GMO, sustainably raised, and fair trade, of course. i can help cook, too, but we just need to stop in downtown San Francisco to get my pots and pans. i refuse to use anything else. These are thimerosal-free.

i AM DEFINITELY NOT A FREELOADER. i will repay you with Reiki massage, and i will give a complimentary lecture to the camp on Flat Earth (i have an honorary degree in the subject from Trump University).

See you on the Playa! Peace and love! Manifest love and light to the youniverse!! ⛆🜨🜔✳🝡✦☆🜏☺🜍☻☢🝮🏠🏚🖼

DJ Ass Maggots Goes to Italy

After spending three hours on the phone with American Express Platinum Concierge, DJ Ass Maggots opts not to spend $9,000 on a business-class flight to Italy and instead buys an $850 bottom-of-the-barrel coach ticket and vows to use that saved money for lavish hotel rooms and charity.

That's it. i also saved money on this story by not writing it . . .

You LOVE Money (A Diss Track)

"Money is the root of all evil."

But you don't believe that. You shallow, insecure, small man. Your lack of insight, combined with your provincial worldview, puts you in a predictable place. Your envy and vindictiveness make you petty.

Oh, but you LOVE money. You don't have as much of it as you pretend to have, but you love that lifestyle. You love to surround yourself with affluent people. You love to discuss Patek Philippe watches, Porsches, beach homes, but you really can't afford any of it. But as long as you know someone who can, you'll try to squeeze your skinny fat-kid body in.

But guess what? i'm going to show you the evil in money. i'm going to show you how someone with money can hire a lawyer to sue you. It doesn't matter if there's a legitimate case. Just being sued requires legal protection. That costs money—money that you don't have, check-to-check pretender. Dirtbag drifter. Deadbeat dad. i'm going to sue for every frivolous and ridiculous thing i can imagine until you're bankrupt. My pocket goes ten times deeper than your pocket, and i have ten times as many pockets.

Do you know how much a private investigator costs? Don't answer—because you can't afford one anyway. It's amazing what dirt people can dig up. Internet searches, twenty-four-hour surveillance, home searches, fiber-optic cameras.

Now let's talk about hit men. Or rather, let's not. The only leverage you have left is the ability to try to report me to law enforcement. For someone who claims to hate cops, you sure do like to call them. Do you know it costs $50,000 to REDACTED someone. Of course you do, because i told you that. And you still want to play? You are an idiot. Perhaps a mental midget. You're like a special-needs mouse, and i'm a lion, just kicking you around, bored.

Anyway, i don't need to do any of this. Because you are destroying yourself faster than i could ever destroy you. Keep it up, black hole. Soul sucker.

By the way, remember when you said your girlfriend was as tight as a dime? You're right. She was. And so were your children.

Enjoy that visual. And enjoy your one-way ticket to the Bronx, Dennis the Menace, Munoz 3.0. Bart Simpson's big mouth trapped in Homer Simpson's body. i hope you live forever, because death would be compassionate.

No matter how hard you try, you are not me.

You bee-lined toward me from your miserable existence with your hungry eyes, but your money wasn't on point.

i should have never let you in my house.

As Bob Marley said, "You running and you running and you running away, but you can't run away from yourself."

Jailbreak Your Brain

So this raver walks up to me . . .

"Yo, can I get some molly?"

"Sure. Twenty a pop."

"Done."

"Who's next?"

An anorexic blonde comes up. "Me. Me. Got any blow?"

"Sure. Sixty a gram."

"Sixty! I only got twenty."

"Beat it. Who's next?"

"Hey, do you got anything different?"

"Sure. Shrooms, acid, Special K."

"Sweet. I'll take an ounce of shrooms."

"OK. Go with my buddy here round back. Who's next?"

There is only one person left in line. This Malaysian girl. Mighty Malaysian. "Do you have anything really different?"

"Good question. Whaddaya want? Uppers? downers? Sideways? Lasers?"

"Something really different."

"Wanna unlock your brain?"

"What do you mean?"

"Well, this might be a little complicated . . . so there are parts of your body that kind of work on their own. Like your liver, pancreas, adrenal glands, neurotransmitters in your brain . . . you take this, and you can control it."

"What the fuck! How?"

"Do you know what a suppository is?"

"Isn't that something you put up your butt?"

"You got it! You gotta use the applicator. Put it just in your butt. Just inside. Then squirt. The lotion will absorb into your rectal mucosa, and then into your bloodstream."

"Then what happens?"

"The chemicals will bind to your red blood cells. Then, they'll go to the target and do whatever they're supposed to do. For example, the pineal extract will unlock your pineal gland. That's like literally opening your third eye. But that might be a little crazy. Better to start with AdrenoHack. That gives you a little adrenal rush. On demand."

"Aren't you worried that I might be a cop?"

"That is fucking ho-larious. First of all, this is Area 33. Culver City Vice has already been taken care of. Second of all, cops don't ask for something 'different.' They want the usual shit. And a lot of it. On the first buy. When you decided to go beyond psychedelics, you piqued my interest."

"You thought of all that just now?"

"Kind of. i took Sympathy before i came out. It's a substance that affects the sympathetic nervous system generally, so i'm just kind of charged up all over. Like an espresso. My pupils are a little bit dilated, my mouth is dry, my heartbeat is fast, my lungs are breathing deep, my digestion is slowed, my blood sugar is up, my bathroom needs are on hold. Classic 'flight-or-fight' adrenaline response. But just a little. Just enough to be sharp. Sharper than you. Sharper than anyone."

"Like that movie *Limitless*!"

"Yeah, kind of . . . except that was about a magical fictional pill that makes you 'all that you can be.' The human body is much more complicated than that. Just being hyperaware all the time is taxing. And in that movie, they became addicted to it. It was a drug. This is simply using molecular biology to tap into your already existing organs. And actually, i know a guy who is trying to integrate it into a computer network."

The Malaysian girl gives me a sarcastic look. "What. The. Fuck? OK. Am I on *Punk'd* or something?"

"Ha ha . . . listen. i'm heading back to my estate. Jump in my Lamborghini, and i'll tell you about it on the way."

"What? Ummmm . . . I came with some friends. And I live in Pomona."

"Pomona! What are you doing out in the sticks? Well, your decision. Well . . . at least for now. At least until i get a remote control for your body. Picture me turning down your volume, turning up your horniness, turning off your inhibitions. That's what this guy is doing. Except, instead of a remote control, he's doing it over Wi-Fi on an iPad app."

"Fuck my friends. I'm going with you!"

Rush Hours

With traffic this bad, i can text out a quick story while i crawl along at 5 mph in this Friday-evening 405 Freeway commuting hell. Look at all the sad-faced zombies trudging back to their homes after another monotonous work week. Whatever victory the unions achieved in getting the eight-hour workday have gradually been lost, as we are now back to the twelve-hour workday if you factor in the commute.

Future generations who will undoubtedly be magnetic and electric mass-transit powered will look back at this time with wonderment at the complete failure of human transportation engineering and with disgust at the rabid avarice of oil companies. Here we are: arrogant, scientific, technologically advanced human beings, suckered into generations of gas-guzzling, atmosphere-polluting, metal-contraption automobiles all leaving work at the same time.

Who killed the electric car?

Why is it called "rush hour" anyway? Traffic is pretty much jammed from 3:00 p.m. until 7:00 p.m. Seems more than an hour to me.

Well, i fit right in today with my Dodge Charger rental. Inconspicuous. i am nobody. i look at the cars next to me. Nobody is looking at me.

Sunset on the 405. How many times have you gathered with strangers on the beach to watch a sunset? Whereas here, we are all gathered alone in our cars on the freeway to watch the sun descend right onto the road. Violaceous tangerine sun rays. Pollution makes the most beautiful sunsets.

No nice cars out here on this dusk patrol. The rich don't commute? Los Angeles is definitely stratified into its economic classes. The poor take the bus. The middle class travel for hours in their cars. And the rich don't commute. i don't see any Rolls-Royces or Lamborghinis out here.

i pass two guys standing outside their two Camrys on the right shoulder, exchanging information. i take a close look for damage. Nothing. Pathetic. Then i get closer to the main accident. It appears to be on the OTHER side of the freeway! Then why is this side going so slow? Well, as i get closer, i slow down so that i can see the damage and maybe an injury. While i'm stretching my neck to get a closer look, i slam into the car in front of me. Oh shit, i better get off my phone . . .

(completely texted into a phone while driving)

Remote Control

"Television is not the truth! Television is a goddamned amusement park, that's what television is! Television is a circus, a carnival, a traveling troupe of acrobats and storytellers, singers and dancers, jugglers, sideshow freaks, lion tamers and football players. We're in the boredom-killing business!"

—*Network* (1976)

Two Silly Putty–like aliens flying through space on a joyride in a stolen spacecraft came across a small mudhole of a planet and decided to take a closer look.

"Hey, Gumby, look at that little dumpy shithole planet there. According to Google Maps, that is Earth. Looks like it's post-nuked."

"Nah, nah, Pokey. It's pre-nuked. Those 'Earthlings' are just dirty. Remember that planet we saw in the M87 Galaxy of the Virgo Cluster? Now *that* planet was destroyed. All from splitting atoms. Subintellectuals for sure."

Pokey laughed. "How is it that those Earthlings haven't blown themselves up yet trying to split atoms? I mean, building on uranium to make more and more unstable atoms, then splitting it? Who does that? Morons! And they even eat animal flesh. Primitive . . ."

Gumby moved his green right-upper extremity over some controls, then responded, "Well, I try to give them the benefit of the doubt. They might figure out that they control their own gravity. Ahhh, yes, gravity the seducer. Inhaling O_2, then splitting that simple bond and using the flatulence from that burst of energy to propel yourself through the air. All done by focusing the mind on it. They have only learned to fly with their ridiculous contraptions for a hundred Earth years or so. They might figure it out. Gravity is literally 'all in the mind.'"

"Hell no, Gumby. I say they're morons. Let's go down there and scoop a bunch of them up. I need some new remote controls."

"Do you really want to? You clearly don't remember, but we've been there before. It was about forty Earth years ago. Remember? We thought *they* thought *we* were gODs. They started making models of us. Very realistic, actually. Almost as bendable and stretchy as us. They even had the right shade of your orange and my green. Then it turned out they were just using them as toys for their children."

Pokey looked nonplussed. "Wait a minute . . . I remember that! That was Earth? Oh man, I hate that place. It was like talking to a wall. They still believe gOD floats around in space. They look everywhere for gOD except internally. Screw them! Let's go pick up a few remote controls. At least they're good for that!"

Gumby chuckled. "Funny thing is, Pokey, they actually have handheld devices to control their televisions and some other appliances, and they call those devices 'remote controls.' I wonder when they will figure out that *they*, in fact, are the ones being controlled remotely BY their televisions. Everything they do is from their TVs. Their thoughts, their clothes, their politics, religion. One of their own even made a movie called *Network* that brought attention to it. But no one saw it. Silly, silly creatures."

"But they are great remote controls," Pokey eagerly interjected. "I had one in my house for a while. Greeeaat! You could tell them anything, make them do anything. All with simple threats. They respond so well to fear. So simple. I had one doing all kinds of chores. Even washed all three of my anuses daily. I totally controlled him, just by shooting his foot off. He couldn't even figure out how to self-regenerate it. After that, he did whatever I wanted. Best remote controls this side of galaxy cluster Abell 3627. For suuure."

"Fuck it," Gumby acquiesced. "Pokey, when you're right, you're right. Let's do this, homey."

American Psycho Book Report

Modern masterpiece! Bret Easton Ellis describes this 416-page book (fourteen-CD audiobook) that he finished in 1991 as "autobiographical, except for the killing and stuff." i had seen the movie but hadn't heard much about the book. Like everyone else in our couch-potato, mindless-consumer, zombie society, i had not even considered *reading* a worthwhile hobby until a year ago. Sure, sure, i read plenty as a kid and in school. Whatevs . . . leave me alone, Dad! Come on, i mean, i'm doing a voluntary book report!

Apparently, there was supposed to be an *American Psycho: The Musical*!

This *is* going inside the mind of a true sociopath.

"I was living like Patrick Bateman. I was slipping into a consumerist kind of void that was supposed to give me confidence and make me feel good about myself but just made me feel worse and worse and worse about myself," Ellis said.

"Whether any of the crimes depicted in the novel actually happened or whether they were simply the fantasies of a delusional psychotic is deliberately left open."

"Murders and executions" as "mergers and acquisitions."

"Ellis received numerous death threats and hate mail after the publication of *American Psycho*."

"In Germany, the book was deemed 'harmful to minors,' and its sales and marketing were severely restricted from 1995 to 2000."

"Feminist activist Gloria Steinem was among those opposed to the release of Ellis's book because of its portrayal of violence toward women. Steinem is also the stepmother of Christian Bale, who played Bateman in the film."

Ellis said, "*American Psycho* was a book I didn't think needed to be turned into a movie," as "the medium of film demands answers," which would make the book "infinitely less interesting."

"Though Ellis made his debut at 21 with the controversial 1985 bestseller *Less Than Zero*, a zeitgeist novel about amoral young people in Los Angeles, the work he is most known for is his third novel, 1991's *American Psycho*. On its release, the literary establishment widely condemned the novel as overly violent and misogynistic; though many petitions to ban the book saw Ellis dropped by Simon & Schuster, the resounding controversy made it a paperback bestseller for Alfred A. Knopf later that year."

From *American Psycho*:

[T]here is an idea of a Patrick Bateman, some kind of abstraction, but there is no real me, only an entity, something illusory, and though I can hide my cold gaze and you can shake my hand and feel flesh gripping yours and maybe you can even sense our lifestyles are probably comparable: I simply am not there. It is hard for me to make sense on any given level. Myself is fabricated, an aberration. I am a noncontingent human being. My personality is sketchy and unformed, my heartlessness goes deep and is persistent. My conscience, my pity, my hopes disappeared a long time ago (probably at Harvard) if they ever did exist.

There are no more barriers to cross. All I have in common with the uncontrollable and the insane, the vicious and the evil, all the mayhem I have caused and my utter indifference toward it, I have now surpassed. I still, though, hold on to one single bleak truth: no one is safe, nothing is redeemed. Yet I am blameless. Each model of human behavior must be assumed to have some validity. Is evil something you are? Or is it something you do?

My pain is constant and sharp and I do not hope for a better world for anyone. In fact, I want my pain to be inflicted on others. I want no one to escape. But even after admitting this—and I have countless times, in just about every act I've committed—and coming face-to-face with these truths, there is no catharsis. I gain no deeper knowledge about myself, no new understanding can be extracted from my telling. There has been no reason for me to tell you any of this. This confession has meant nothing.

Burner Real Estate

"So you want some Burner property? I'll tell you what, I can put you in a nice two-bedroom space behind Center Camp, quick access to 6:00 and C, ice and coffee within walking distance."

"Are you kidding me? i don't want that downtown ghetto crap! That's right next to the Black Hole. Do you have any idea what kind of shit i'll have to put up with every night? How 'bout a nice theme camp spot in Distrikt Heights, 9:30 and F, with a view of the Man?"

"Well . . . there's nothing like that available right now, but I can put you in a high-rise at 2:30 and J with full views of the Man, Deep Playa, and the Temple, with quick access to Opulent Temple. You might be able to get on the Dildo King's art car."

"J? i'm not staying out in the sticks! i can room with some people at Playa Surfers. They're on the Esplanade!"

(Laughing) "Let's be realistic. You don't know anyone in Playa Surfers, and name-dropping won't help. What's next—you're Larry Harvey's nephew? Look, I'll just put you in DPW. You don't have to pay for admittance. You'll have backstage

access. You just have to stick around another month after to clean up."

(Groans) "Fuck this. Burning Man was better last year. i'm just gonna go to Coachella."

Gas Station

"Instead of eating exclusively from the sun, humanity now began to sip petroleum."
—Michael Pollan, *The Omnivore's Dilemma:*
A Natural History of Four Meals

Liquidity. Gasolina. Drops of carbon rings attached octagonally drip . . . drip . . . drip. Don't top off. Going to get gas is our dirty little secret, like going to the bathroom. We don't need to talk about it. i don't want to know your dirty little secrets. You filthy whore.

Mom.

Earth.

"I'm on a diet, so I'll have a Diet Coke." My car is on a diet, so i fill it up with UN-leaded. UN. United Nations. Supreme UNleaded, regular UNleaded, and that middle one. And diesel. And nachos, why not?

i'm just trying to make a quick stop at the gas station. i didn't think i would get shot. Got robbed. Got my wallet. Got my plastic. Plaaaaaastic. Plaaaaastique. It's explosive. It's carbon.

Blood. Earth's blood. "Wash your hands. You smell like gas." Maybe you should wash your butt—*you* smell like gas. The other gas.

You can trace a drop of oil around the Earth. Ask Michael Pollan. He wrote a book.

i went to the gas station today. i only put twenty bucks in. Just enough to get me around town and to the ATM, where i'll take out another twenty bucks. Round and around. rOund anD aRoUnd. rouNd aNd arounD. RounD AnD ArounD. rOuNd aNd aRouNd.

i'm a discriminating shopper. i go where gas is cheaper. Even if it is far away. Even if it dangerous. Gas is cheaper in the hood. Poor people make cheaper gas.

This Space Available for Advertising. Chevwrong— Making the Children of Tomorrow.

Don't smoke at the gaaaaaas station. That's dangerous. But smoking on your own is fine. We don't care about *you*. We just don't want anything to happen to the gaaaaaas station.

Texaco sounds like *Mexico*. *Exxon* sounds like *Chevron* sounds like *Enron*. *Environ*. Environmental Protection Agency. EPA. DEA. CIA.

Shell must be from the ocean. Clean coal.

Special-interest group.

Service at the gaaaaaaas station. You are getting served. Fully. Selflessly. Don't talk on your cell phone at the gaaaaaas station. That's dangerous. Brain tumors are *your* problem. We just don't want anything to happen to the gaaaaas station.

Mad Max. Mad Men. Mad dam. *Saddam* backward is *Mad ass*.

JFK likes petrol. Khadafi. Petrol dollars.

Gas is natural. Natural gas. You just fracked up.

You ever drink a drop of gas? You ever get some in your eye? Toxic poison. But it is you.

No blood for oil? Well, maybe a little. Everyone likes vampires. Maybe a little bit more blood. (whisper) *Maybe a bit more oil.*

IRAQ. IRAN. IRA. RAN. AN. AND. OBAMA AND BIDEN. OSAMA BIN LADEN.

Carbon tax party.

You are funny. You are a gas. You are chaos. Gas is cash. Gas is chaos.

This story is based on Homer's *Odyssey* and is divided into eighteen episodes.

Tertiary butylhydroquinone chick'n nuggets.

Fossil fuel. Six-hundred-fifty-million-year-old dinosaur bone juice. Freak gasoline fight accident.

Drink shit, drive shit, shit shit.

Fossil fuel to fuel us fossils. Dinosaur excrement and semen. Carbons melting back into our Mother. Reanimated corpses are we, shooting projectile rocket explosives at each other from thousands of miles away in a battle over dinosaur juice.

THIS SPACE FOR RENT BY VIACOM (one eye winking)

Clear channel. Clearly.

If you really want to SEE what's going on, CLOSE YOUR EYES.

Italian Girl

"Tu sei come una pietra preziosa che viene violentemente frantumata in mille schegge per poter essere ricostruita di una materiale più duraturo di quello della vita, cioè il materiale della poesia." (You're like a precious stone that is violently shattered into a thousand pieces to be rebuilt in a more durable material than life, the material of poetry.)

—Pasolini

Forza Italia, my baby boo
Five years now i know you,
Canadian Italian but then you switched
New York to LA you a bad bitch,
Dreams of you my entire life
Posters on my wall of future wife,
Warmed up with the German version (Porsche)
i'm not your first Persian,
High maintenance
Often on vacation,
Met you in New York, April 5, 2008
Love at first date,

Brought you out to LA
Still just as wrinkleless today,
Wrapping splashes of screams
Mercilessly give my life meaning,
Italian Riviera along the coast
Only the two of us never alone . . .
Damn you, Geoffrey Chaucer! i've had it with your 1390 AD
outdated Canterbury couplets!
You cannot constrain love!
James Joyce, take me home!
Squeeeal spinnn. Not using protection.
Brrrrrrr and *arrrrrrrrr* and *mmmmmmm.*
Different sounds in sex positions.
European size 19 head-turning shoes.
Love horses 400. Reckless.
Not afraid to burp or fart out a little gas when i squeeze you.
Screeeeam!
i open you up to reveal your inner Burgundy.
Mascarpone, Italian ices,
Prancing ponies.
Italian Riviera—Sanremo, Savona, Genoa, La Spezia.
Along the Mediterranean,
Then the Adriatic,
Thousands of miles of coast.
Only the two of us, so i am never alone.
We sit naked together, and i wash your beautiful backside.
You are a wide body, but i would never call you fat.
Every guy wants to be *in* you.
You squeal when i touch you.

Finicky, fragile, but a wild whip.
Enzo. Stradale, Modena.
Scuderia.
Real girl hardly,
You are my car bella Ferrari.

Henry Miller's Black Spring (1936)

"The smell of horse piss and lion's dung, of tiger's breath and elephant's hide. Obscenity, lust, cruelty, boredom, wit. Real eunuchs. Real hermaphrodites. Real pricks. Real cunts . . ."

"I never realized that a whole world could be diseased!"

"Out of the leaking mains love gushing like sewer gas: furious love with black gloves and bright bits of garter, love that champs and snorts, love hidden in a barrel and blowing the bunghole night after night."

"And all might have gone beautifully for him had he not fallen for a red-haired walk-on who was rotting away with syphilis. That finished him."

"If you could take a penny from your pocket and balance the books you would do so. But you are no longer dealing with actual pennies. There is no machine clever enough to devise, to counterfeit, this penny which does not exist. The world of real and counterfeit is behind us. Out of the tangible we have invented the intangible."

"If we are stirred by a fat bust it is the fat bust of a whore who bent over on a rainy night and showed us for the first time the wonder of the great milky globes."

"There are passages in 'Ulysses' which can be read only in the toilet—if one wants to extract the full flavor of their content."

"Yes I said and I thought to myself what a sap you've been to wait so long. She was so wet and juicy down there, and so childlike, so trustful, why anybody could have come along and had what's what. She was a pushover."

"*The plague!* The plague of modern progress: colonization, trade, free Bibles, war, disease, artificial limbs, factories, slaves, insanity, neuroses, psychoses, syphilis, tuberculosis, anemia, strikes, lockouts, starvation, nullity, vacuity, restlessness, striving, despair, ennui, suicide bankruptcy, arteriosclerosis, megalomania, schizophrenia, hernia, cocaine, prussic acid, stink bombs, tear gas, mad dogs, auto-suggestion, auto-intoxication, psychotherapy, hydrotherapy, electric massages, vacuum cleaners, pemmican, grapenuts, hemorrhoids, gangrene. No desert isles. No Paradise. Not even relative happiness. Men running away from themselves so frantically that they look for salvation under the ice floes or in tropical swamps, or else they climb the Himalayas or asphyxiate themselves in the stratosphere."

"No more peeping through holes! No more masturbating in the dark! ... I want a world where the vagina is represented by a crude, honest slit, a world that has feeling for bone and contour, for raw, primary colors, a world that has fear and respect for its animal origins. I'm sick of looking at cunts all tickled up, disguised, deformed, idealized. Cunts with nerve ends exposed. I don't want to watch young virgins masturbating in the privacy of their boudoirs or biting their nails or tearing their hair or lying on a bed full of breadcrumbs for a whole chapter. I want Madagascan funeral poles, with animal upon animal and at the top Adam and Eve, and Eve with a crude, honest slit between the legs. I want hermaphrodites who are real hermaphrodites, and not make-believes walking around with an atrophied penis or a dried-up cunt. I want a classic purity, where dung is dung and angels are angels."

"She slept with everybody, except her own husband."

"The King James Version was created by a race of bone-crushers. It revives the primitive mysteries, revives rape, murder, incest, revives epilepsy, sadism, megalomania, revives demons, angels, dragons, leviathans, revives magic, exorcism, contagion, incantation, revives fratricide, regicide, patricide, suicides, revives hypnotism, anarchism, somnambulism, revives the song, the dance, the act, revives the mantic, the chthonian, the arcane, the mysterious, revives the power, the evil, and the glory that is God."

"Everybody's getting ready to get raped, drugged, violated, soused with the new music that seeps out of the sweat of the asphalt."

"Ought to stand on Times Square with my pecker in my hand and piss in the gutter. Ought to grab a revolver and fire point-blank into the crowd."

"We'd eat our own dung and that nice new fetus Jill's got inside her."

"In the past every member of our family did something with his hands. I'm the first idle son of a bitch with a glib tongue and a bad heart."

"You start out with the sublime and you end up in an alley jerking away for dear life."

"You are about to write a beautiful book and in it you are going to record everything that has given you pain or joy."

"The great artist is he who conquers the romantic in himself."

My End of Watch Movie Review for Fifth Period, Eleventh Grade, Mr. Dudool Homeroom

Hi, everyone, my name is Sara Deevaneh, and here is my review of *End of Watch*, a 2012 American thriller/drama film starring *my lover*, Jake Gyllenhaal, and some Mexican guy, Michael Peña, as LAPD officers who work in South-Central Los Angeles.

First of all, I'm glad that they acknowledged the corporate sponsors in the beginning. My dad works for NBC Universal, so he was happy. Also, since Jake Gillenhaal spent much of his own money (executive producer), he must have known it would be a good movie.

I really liked how it showed cops as the good guys, which is the way it is. Not like those weird older movies, *Colors* and *Training Day*, which show "bad cops," which my dad says is not realistic.

Even though I don't know much about Mexicans (I'm Persian, from Beverly Hills), I thought it was cool (and pretty accurate) how Michael Peña took off his gun and stuff and fought that black gangster guy toe-to-toe in his own house. Of course the cop won! Yay!

I'm not really a rap fan, but I did enjoy the one rap song in the movie by Chuck D. I've never heard of him. He must be new and probably a big fan of the police.

This movie showed many violent and dangerous black and Latino people in really, really bad parts of town—Compton, I guess—doing terrible things like tying up children and illegal immigration. Since the most dangerous place going south I've ever been is Culver City, I had to ask my dad if it was accurate. He said it was. Plus, I knew it was realistic because they used handheld cameras and stuff to film it.

Jake Gullenhall is *such* a good actor. I could totally tell it was him right away, so I knew everything would be OK.

Honestly, I haven't seen cops this cool since *Miami Vice*. Yes, the movie, not the TV show! How old *are* you?!! FYI, *The A-Team* movie is also excellent (I totally didn't even know there was a show 😊!)

I'm also glad they mentioned Starbucks and Red Bull, because I also drink them (right now, as a matter of fact!). Jake Gillynhall even says "Drink more coffee" in the movie! Yay!

The military guy looked tough and cool. I hope my brother joins the navy!

I really enjoyed how the movie transformed into a romantic comedy. The two couples both getting married was sooo sweet!

Spoiler alert: I cried when I thought Jake Gilllenhaaal died, but then they became tears of joy when he survived and only the Mexican partner died. I guess that's kind of sad too.

Well, that's it for now, everyone. I have to go help my dad shave his back. *Ciao!*

Hole

Oocytes float through the tight, dimly lit cavern as she holds her girlfriend's hand and goes deeper. Spiritual tantric grooves light the kundalini sequence. Several butterflies on yoga mats stretch, massage each other. Tribal subwoofers bellow bass in our chests as couples embrace. Smiling.

Ninth Street and Main.

Shoes in cubbyholes, sock-footed prancing, i am overwhelmed by the abundant gratitude of Sister Earthlings. Gypsy darling soft-hopping with shadows. Psychedelic downtempo.

Booommmmmmmmmm.

Ahmmmmmmmmmm.

Ommmmmmmmmmmmmmmmmmmmmmmmmm.

More limber than before, i reach my toes, breeeeeathe.

A man with eyeliner and dreads steps onto a bench and starts rapping, trapping to the bass-heavy delicious chunks of sound in this candlelit hall:

Hello people, it is I, the King,
Representing Man,
Bowing down to the Queens,
Representing these Underlands.

Upstairs now, raw vegan delicacies prepared for feathered fluffy rabbits on barstools. Mother Earth herself behind the counter, offering up free samples of "tangerine-like, dehydrated peachy things" (great description, Tyson) in a juice.

Indian woman, you capture my heart every time. The eyes do the dancing. The eyes hypnotize. Siren, the seducer.

As the minimal techno house music pumps sound blood through the air, i disintegrate . . .

I AM ELECTRIC.

(written on location at Peace Yoga,
Ninth and Main, LA)

Unicorny

She stares at the unlabeled, unbubbled bottled water sitting on the table at Bouchon Bistro, a stylish upstairs Beverly Hills hideaway dripping in burgundy, maroon, crimson, and candlelight, wondering if she made the right choice going out to dinner tonight with this mysterious guy. Auntie Shaling would most definitely not approve of this strange man.

"I think he only wants to sleep with me," she thinks.

"Where did you say you're from again?" she asks.

"I didn't." He laughs mysteriously. "I'm American."

"Duh, I know that, silly. We're all American, but where are you *originally* from? For example, I'm from Hong Kong."

"Ahh, yes. A tough question. I am . . . Middle Eastern."

"I thought so! Persian?"

"Not exactly, even though I am hairy enough."

They both laugh. A unibrowed gentleman at the next table whispers disapprovingly in Farsi to his date.

"No, seriously, where are you from?" she asks again, smile gone.

A waitress brings out a birthday cake from across the room as a group at a big table starts singing "Happy Birthday."

Everyone is smiling in this place. It's Christmas. It's always Christmas here. Downstairs, people with signs protest bank bailouts.

"I'm a unicorn," he blurts out. "From the planet Unicornia."

She stares blankly for a few seconds, then a huge smile forms. "Amazing! I love unicorns!"

The man looks nonplussed. "I'm not joking."

"In some strange way, I can feel you're telling the truth, or at least you believe you're telling the truth. But if you're a unicorn, where's your horn?"

"I shave it off every morning with special Unicornian clippers. Here—feel the top of my forehead, just at the hairline. Feel that supersoft, satinlike marshmallow stubble? If I let it grow for a week, you will see a full-fledged shiny silver marshmallow unicorn horn."

"Marshmallow? I never knew they were marshmallow."

"Well, you humans don't exactly have the most accurate books on aliens and mythology. I mean, you think aliens all have big oval heads and are always trying to attack Earth. But in reality, you guys are the only violent planet this side of star cluster Nebulon 5."

"Really? Wow. So the universe is filled with aliens?"

"Yes. Oh yes," answers the man with a faraway look as he tries to get some meat out of a trout's cheek with a small tri-pronged shellfish fork. They leave the bistro an hour later and get lost in the parking garage.

"I'm pretty sure your car's this way." She leads, drunk, into a dead end.

"You. Are. Lost," he jokes as he backs her up against a wall and kisses her on the lips.

She bends her right knee and implants her Jimmy Choo heel into the wall. He positions his stance in between her slightly parted legs and kisses her again, more aggressively this time, biting her lower lip. She lets out a little yelp.

"Uni . . . corn, you like it rough, don't you?" She already knows his answer. Before he can respond, she puts a hand on the tent of his crotch. "Someone's ready for business," she remarks as she unzips. A golden light emits. "What the hell?" She probes deeper and pulls out his . . . shiny silver marsh-mallow log. "Oh my g—this is not human!"

"Of course not," he defends. "I'm a unicorn."

Puppets

"Master of puppets I'm pulling your strings
Twisting your mind and smashing your dreams"
—Metallica

"I want some sushi. Not this refrigerator supermarket crap you got here."

My med school colleague Ohms's declaration led to me calling American Express Platinum concierge services and booking a table at Urasawa.

On a Tuesday night about a month later, we head up to Beverly Hills, park in a standard valet parking garage, take an elevator up to a nondescript floor, walk down a hallway past some bathrooms, and enter through some curtains into the Japanese shrine of food. The Timothy Leary, a.k.a. Albert Hofmann, on my tongue begins to kick in.

Every dish is a work of art and a labor of love at Hiro Urasawa's Beverly Hills Japanese—LA's No. 1 for Food—where the sublime omakase-only feasts are prepared by the maestro himself with the utmost attention to detail in a tranquil setting; service is impeccable, too, so put it on your bucket list, but be ready to fork over your car payment for the once-in-a-lifetime treat.

—Zagat

We were in. All in: $488 a person, no menus, a $200 bottle of sake, and room for exactly eight people at the bar. Two couples were already seated. Chinese girls with American guys. Everyone looked up at us as we walked in. i could see the disappointment in one of the Chinese girl's visible thought balloons: "They're nobody."

The master chef, Hiro Urasawa himself, presides over the bar and asks if we have any food allergies. He laughs genuinely when i say Ohms is allergic to sushi. The master also comments on how he likes my shirt, a $200 colorful long-sleeved Custo Barcelona. Ohms in his $2,000 Armani cashmere sweater sulks jealously.

Sure, sure. The food, delicious; the service, royal; the decor, minimal. But so what?

So then Denzel Washington and a couple of buddies walk in. They are seated at a little table separated from us by a glass partition. i couldn't help thinking that even with all the anticelebrity, anti-Hollywood rhetoric that i had been pushing recently, i was still starstruck.

i post all of this on Facebook as the night progresses.

My friend, the Pope, texts me: Denzel Washington hasn't made a good movie in years. Fuck him.

He's right. Although i did kind of want to walk out of the restaurant growling "King Kong ain't got nothing on this place" and give him a "my man!" on the way out.

An hour later, Ohms and i are drunk, and Denzel has moved up to the bar. He appears to be drunk as well. Ohms and i get into a side conversation about celebrity worship.

"Dude, fuck celebrities. They're just puppets, man. Doing a little song and dance," he starts.

"Yeah, but we support this shit. Every time we go to the movies, or buy a DVD, or pay our cable bill, we support this mass BS brainwashing that is Hollywood. That's money that could go to schools or schoolteachers. Why does a teacher make twenty *grand* a year while an actor playing a teacher makes twenty *mil* a year?"

"That's capitalism, baby," he responds. "Three hundred million Americans all lapping this shit up. And the actors aren't even the puppet masters. They're just employees. The real money is in the studios and the networks that pay them."

He was right, and i was pissed. "Man, we could shut this whole facade down by just collectively boycotting Hollywood. In one year alone, Americans could take care of all our public education needs by just directing that money into the schools."

Ohms challenged me. "So you want to stop watching movies and TV for a year and give that money to the government and wait for them to distribute it to schools? That will be popular."

i was depressed.

A little later and a little drunker, everyone at the bar gets into anecdotes. Ohms starts telling Denzel and company about one of his paranoid pseudobiology associates who thinks everyone is trying to sleep with his girl. He gets a round of laughs. Denzel's perfect teeth and resonating bellow are important to me.

One of the Chinese girls asks if there are any parties tonight. i put out a text to my main man and club promoter in Hollywood, Buster. He responds in ten minutes: Bootsy Bellows.

Suddenly, the once-in-a-lifetime Urasawa experience becomes old news, and now it's time to step it up a gear. Ohms pays for the entire bill, about $1,400, despite my protests. It's Nowruz, the Persian New Year, after all.

We get to Sunset Boulevard and Doheny and see a huge line. Buster is there to greet us and directs our brand-new supercharged Range Rover toward the valet. We easily bypass the paparazzi circus outside, and my Amex Platinum and driver's license disappear into the all-too-accepting hands of the hostess. Gulp.

After discussing different champagne choices and the $1,500 minimum, we are seated at an oversize table at the back of the club. One of the gimmicks of this place is that they have a bunch of marionette puppets on strings with people controlling them, walking around and entertaining the guests. The puppets appear to be the Rolling Stones. Next to our table, a guy handling a hideous miniature Mick Jagger dances out of our way.

"More puppets," Ohms mumbles. i wonder if he's talking about us or the marionettes.

Buster introduces me to David Arquette, who happens to be one of the owners of this new hotspot.

"This is my brain surgeon," Buster impresses David.

"He's incurable," i joke. David laughs.

i whisper to Ohms, "That's the guy from *Friends*."

"He's not on *Friends*. He's in the *Scary Movie* movies."

"Whatever."

One of the club promoters tells us it's OK to smoke cigarettes in here. Wow. This place is racy. Then comes the champagne, fireworks, and dancing girls.

"Happy New Year," i tell Ohms. Then i announce to the girls, "It's Ohms's birthday!" They all ooo and ahhh.

i start talking to a psychologist in a miniskirt with a feigned snobby-Valley-girl accent.

"So, like, I'm from San Franciscooo. The people are soo much cooler there—"

"Hella cool," i interrupt.

"Yeah, totally. Everyone here is so shallow and fake. Who cares about celebrities anyway? What-*ever*."

"But you're sitting right in the middle of the hottest Hollywood club, surrounded by celebrities. Shouldn't you be contemplating this while meditating in a forest? Anyways, it's not slime. It's just young people having a good time," i philosophize.

"It's kind of loud in here, and I can't really hear what you're saying," she continues. "I'm twenty-nine, and I totally am into my career and stuff."

"Where do you work?"

"Well, I'm waiting to finish some classes so I can get into a psychology department."

i tell her i'm the surgeon general. She nods approvingly.

Later, the waitress tricks me into buying another bottle of champagne, which comes with a fire-breathing dancing lady. Later, i find out that the total bill comes to $2,200. i should have paid for dinner.

It's amazing how all the bottle-vampire girls crowded around us when the champagne arrived and how smoothly they snuck away when the bottle was empty.

Now it's 2:00 a.m., and the club is over. Lights come on, and we all start filing toward the door. Since we just spent a shitload of money and have a table next to the celebrity owner, security lets us hang out until 2:15 a.m. Roughly two hours of partying for $2,000. i think i can feel puppet strings coming out of my ass.

Outside the club is the usual paparazzi pandemonium. The girl GG (Golnesa) from the TV show *Shahs of Sunset* walks by with a coat over her head, led by her body-guard. Will.i.am and some other Black Eyed Peas come out, and the photogs buzz and follow them. i start filming the paparazzi. They give me dirty looks. The irony is that celebrities hate the paparazzi, who make a living selling pictures to magazines that their very own fans purchase, keeping them in business. In effect, the celebrities really hate their fans.

The valet takes forever to find our car. We are the actual last people to leave the garage. By then, the celebrities, the pretty girls, the club promoters, and the paparazzi are all gone. It's just Ohms and me and our full stomachs. i start to feel sick and walk a bit down the sidewalk and begin vomiting on some unknown Hollywood star on the Walk of Fame. i go down on a knee. How ironic. In ancient times, people worshiped the stars in the sky. Now we worship the stars on the ground.

"Blacklight Sleaze" by Peace Division

Sometimes, I wonder what I'm doing here
In the middle of this tiny square room
Filled with smoke and damp carpet
Soggy with spilled cheap champagne
With the mirrors and flashing lights
And plastic bowls half-full of salted peanuts
In their discarded shells.
And this room with tired waitresses
Lousy, overpriced drinks
Into the black . . .
I feel sorry for the men sometimes
Mostly I just feel contempt
The men with their furtive movements and blank faces
I feel sorry for Stacey
Her face looks as though it's been stepped on
Though her body is like angel food
Almost too beautiful to look at
Her boyfriend probably doesn't when he hits her
I feel sorry for Lynne

With her expensive lingerie
Cheap dime-store wigs
Trying to hide her identity
She's a Yale graduate with a huge loan debt
She hooks a little on the side
I feel sorry for Babette
With her hennaed Cleopatra hair
And large luminous eyes
Her adorable accent of broken English
Can't hide her drug habit and predatory nature
Into the black . . .
Sometimes I wonder what I'm doing here
Dancing naked except for a few sequins
Lying to men for drink commissions
I take their room keys and make promises I know I won't
fulfill
We're all victims in one way or another
We're all here for different reasons
Sometimes I wonder what I'm doing here
I like to sleep all day and stay out all night
The idea of a straight job is like the idea of a straitjacket
I like buying clothes
I like taking taxis
I'm pretty and intelligent
Sarcastic and selfish
I'm not going to be doing this forever
Into the black . . .
And I'm not going to be doing this forever
I'm only 18.

North Korea

i wrote this in 2013. Still accurate.

Just finished watching National Geographic's *Inside North Korea* (2006). Just like Anderson Cooper's recent report, it showed the terrible conditions inside this totalitarian country, from poor health care to prison camps; from brainwashed citizens to lack of basic supplies. i'm sure all of this is true, and i'm not trying to dispute it or spread misinformation.

What bothers me is the fearmongering and mass hypnosis that these reports perpetuate. All of a sudden everyone is talking about North Korea, from all the news channels to doctors in the dining room. The underlying assumption is that there is a humanitarian crisis in which the United States must intervene. The fifty-minute program ends with a video clip of North Korean missiles being fired.

Haven't we fallen for this before? Weapons of mass destruction? Sound familiar? Over four thousand American soldiers dead and hundreds of thousands of Iraqis (large number of civilians) dead. Vietnam? To stop Communism? Over sixty thousand Americans dead and millions of Vietnamese dead.

i'm not trying to be an instigator. All i'm asking is for people to turn off their TVs, or at least stop perpetuating the latest enemy du jour. What happened to Iran and all the other Middle Eastern terrorists? Syria? Can we rotate back to the Russians for at least another Rocky movie?

i have absolutely *no fear* of a nuclear war. If that day ever comes, we are all toast, and there is no sense worrying about it. Wanna buy a bomb shelter?

What is new in North Korea? A missile test? They have been testing missiles for decades. So what. Kim Jong-un? Who knows . . . ask Dennis Rodman.

We will never invade North Korea because they already have nukes and are backed by China and Russia. The best thing that can happen is they screw up and open their border, and North Koreans flood into South Korea, just like Germany in 1989. No, Reagan/Bush did not bring down the Berlin Wall.

Anyway, go back to your TV . . . or maybe reread Orwell's *1984*. Pieces!

"Militarily, the Party do not fear the external conquest of Oceania [the West]—by either Eastasia [China] or Eurasia [Russia]—because the three super-states are military equals."

—Orwell (*1984*)

North Korea (Again?)

WHEN WAS THE LAST TIME North Korea bombed another country?

WHEN WAS THE LAST TIME North Korea invaded another country?

WHEN WAS THE LAST TIME North Korea organized a coup d'état of a democratically elected leader of another country?

WHEN WAS THE LAST TIME North Korea financed a civil war of another country?

WHEN WAS THE LAST TIME North Korea sold arms to terrorists?

WHEN WAS THE LAST TIME North Korea manufactured and sold poisonous gases?

WHEN WAS THE LAST TIME North Korea destabilized the world economy by deregulating the financial industry?

WHEN WAS THE LAST TIME North Korea allowed multinational corporations to plunder the Earth's resources and destroy the environment?

WHEN WAS THE LAST TIME we blamed another country instead of ourselves?

"Economics 101" by Stacy Herbert

Socialism

You have two cows.
You give one to your neighbor.

Communism

You have two cows.
The state takes both and gives you some milk.

Fascism

You have two cows.
The state takes both and sells you some milk.

Nazism

You have two cows.
The state takes both and shoots you.

Bureaucratism

You have two cows.
The state takes both, shoots one, milks the other, and then throws the milk away.

Traditional Capitalism

You have two cows.

You sell one and buy a bull.

Your herd multiplies, and the economy grows.

You sell them and retire on the income.

Royal Bank of Scotland (Venture) Capitalism

You have two cows.

You sell three of them to your publicly listed company, using letters of credit opened by your brother-in-law at the bank, then execute a debt/equity swap with an associated general offer so that you get all four cows back, with a tax exemption for five cows.

The milk rights of the six cows are transferred via an intermediary to a Cayman Island company secretly owned by the majority shareholder, who sells the rights to all seven cows back to your listed company.

The annual report says the company owns eight cows, with an option on one more. You sell one cow to buy a new president of the United States, leaving you with nine cows. No balance sheet provided with the release.

The public then buys your bull.

Surrealism

You have two giraffes.

The government requires you to take harmonica lessons.

An American Corporation

You have two cows.

You sell one and force the other to produce the milk of four cows.

Later, you hire a consultant to analyze why the cow has dropped dead.

A Greek Corporation

You have two cows. You borrow lots of euros to build barns, milking sheds, hay stores, feed sheds, dairies, cold stores, an abattoir, a cheese unit, and packing sheds.

You still only have two cows.

A French Corporation

You have two cows.

You go on strike, organize a riot, and block the roads because you want three cows.

A Japanese Corporation

You have two cows.

You redesign them so that they are one-tenth the size of an ordinary cow and produce twenty times the milk.

You then create a clever cow cartoon image called a Cowkimona and market it worldwide.

An Italian Corporation

You have two cows, but you don't know where they are. You decide to have lunch.

A Swiss Corporation

You have five thousand cows. None of them belong to you. You charge the owners for storing them.

A Chinese Corporation

You have two cows.

You have three hundred people milking them.

You claim that you have full employment and high bovine productivity.

You arrest the journalist who reported the real situation.

An Indian Corporation

You have two cows.

You worship them.

A British Corporation

You have two cows.

Both are mad.

An Iraqi Corporation

Everyone thinks you have lots of cows.

You tell them that you have none.

No one believes you, so they bomb the shit out of you and invade your country.

You still have no cows, but at least you are now a democracy.

An Australian Corporation

You have two cows.

Business seems pretty good.

You close the office and go for a few beers to celebrate.

A New Zealand Corporation

You have two cows.

The one on the left looks very attractive . . .

—Stacey Herbert

World War You

Who likes the old school? Remember back in the day? i think it was, like, the winter of 2018 . . . that was about fifty years ago. A long time ago, back in the day, we used to go to Au Lac on Monday nights, Monday Night DeLight. i remember it like it was . . . today. (It *is* today!) It was so much fun! Sean Hill was the host. He had that big black afro, and then, decades later, it slowly became a big white fro, and eventually he went bald, but it was still beautiful, and we called him "Fro No Mo'."

Remember Gianni Love? Back in the day, he did all the sound, lights, and mixing. He did this for years, decades. But then one day, somehow, he went deaf and blind, but he still showed up, and he still knew how to work all the controls. It was incredible!

Remember Chef Ito? He ran the whole place, made all the food, that delicious plant-based Asian cuisine, and he took all the pics and posted them on Instagram. Remember how he took that vow of silence? He didn't speak for over ten years, but then one day, he was the lead singer of a death metal band, and he was like "RAH RAH RAH, RAH RAH, RAH RAH RAH!" And that was it. He was speaking again.

And we were all like, OK, cool. Remember all that? That was over fifty years ago.

Now, in the summer of 2069, things are all so much different with the American Civil War II happening. So i like to reflect back, back when life was fun. Back when i took that trip to the Philippines. i remember it like it was last week. (It *was* last week!) Any Filipinos here? Nah? Not one? That's because they're all at the hospital taking care of my patients.

Ah, the Philippines: beautiful culture, beautiful people, beautiful seven thousand islands. The hospitality of Manila, which could be a rough place at times, with armored cars and teenage mothers sleeping on cardboard next to their babies. Even the hardworking people made only five dollars a day, working seven days a week. And there was me, in juxtaposition, staying at five-star luxury resorts on tropical islands: speedboats, snorkeling, kayaking . . . BUT THOSE GOD-DAMN JELLYFISH! They got me in the foot! Scarred for life (well, a couple of weeks). Dear jellyfish, i will never forgive you (already forgotten). But everything else was fine . . . EXCEPT THAT VOLCANO! They canceled my flight! i had to switch my itinerary around. That was very inconvenient!

And what about President Duterte of the Philippines? His War on Drugs . . . if they found you with a little nugget of weed in your pocket, you would end up decapitated in the forest, but it was fine to drink and drive all day long.

The United States had a military base in the Philippines, but in the 1990s (almost eighty years ago), a volcano erupted, the base was forced to close, and the Philippine government decided that the US military did not need to come back.

Which makes me reflect: Remember how the US military was in all these countries around the world? But then when the American Civil War II, Electric Boogaloo, started, they had to bring back all the troops from all these foreign countries. It was crazy! They had to come back so we could all fight each other. It was the red states versus the blue states, small-arms fighting. All those guns, bombs, and bullets that America had shipped out to everywhere else were now turned inward, and we were all in the middle of it. AND THERE WILL NEVER BE A THIRD PARTY! That's one thing you'll learn. Just red and blue states, fighting to the end.

Even North and South Korea just became "Korea," like Vietnam. North Korea just usurped South Korea after the United States left. There wasn't any violence. It was Communist, which kind of sucked, but it had a capitalist economy, just like Vietnam back in 2018.

i used that DJ Ass Maggots time-space-wormhole machine to transport back from fifty years in the future to tell you this story. (In 2069, i am just a floating head.) i sent this out on the social media platform of choice in 2069, Myspace, and a random blogger in Pyongyang, Korea, saw it and messaged me: *Are you still alive? Because I think I just read that Texas just shot the first nuclear missile of Civil War II at California.*

i was like, "No . . . what? Lemme step outside." So i stepped outside Au Lac, Monday Night DeLight, walked out into the middle of First Street, and looked toward East LA, and i saw this . . . mushroom cloud. And i said, "What . . ." And i saw the blast wave moving toward me.

i then took a deep breath, appreciated my wondrous longevity and everything i had ever experienced, and then uttered my final words, for some reason in a Southern accent: "Well, damn . . . Texas nuked California."

(live performance)

Dear John Updike

Back when i attended UCLA, my professors revered you. We read *Roger's Version*, and they ejaculated over your clever angle on the whole *Scarlet Letter* thing. i remember one professor vividly lamenting his inability to ever write the way you do. *Memories of the Ford Administration*, clever. (There are no memories of the Ford administration.) i felt a kinship with your protagonist, President James Buchanan, the only bachelor president. Why did the single guy have to start the Civil War? (He was right before Lincoln.) So now, i come across a collection of your short stories. "Morocco." Another sweet masterpiece: a sheltered American family on an eye-opening road trip to Tangier. Well done.

Now, the story "Varieties of Religious Experience" . . . this is actually why i'm writing this letter in the first place. i realize that you're dead and cannot read this. But you became Christian, so maybe you *can* read this letter, from somewhere in the heaven of cyberspace. So this story is about 9/11. You told it from the point of view of a nice financial analyst in his office, high atop the World Trade Center, working hard at his admirable job, then finding out he's going to die when the building gets hit. He has a last phone call with his loving wife, who can see the tower's smoke from their home in New Jersey. You also told the story from the point of view of the passengers of the United Airlines flight that had to courageously take down their hijacked plane.

All of that is fine. The part that made you look like an old man, as well as a part of the current religious propaganda machine, was your depiction of the hijackers themselves: one scene, prehijacking, in a strip club, drinking alcohol, debasing women, making racist remarks against blacks and Jews.

Besides obvious cartoonish villainization of Muslims and patriotic glamorization of the victims, you generally missed the point, my good sir. You didn't explain why. Why, why, why? What was their motivation? Even now as i write this, we Americans have been victims of yet another Muslim "terrorist" attack at the Boston Marathon. And now that all the facts are in place, the final question the news keeps asking is, Why? Why would someone want to hurt us? Or as King George Bush the Second asked about Muslims, "Why do they hate us?"

Everyone knows the answer, but no one wants to say it. US FOREIGN POLICY IN THE MIDDLE EAST.

As long as we Americans finance soldiers to go kill people, mostly Muslims, in the Middle East, from Iran, Iraq, Afghanistan, Palestine, Syria, and the rest, we will be victims of "blowback," or retaliation. That is natural. That is expected. Every living animal on this planet will try to defend itself when attacked. Mr. Updike, you didn't touch on any of this. Instead, you took the easy road of jingoism.

Anyway, i've ranted long enough. Peace or pieces . . .

You should have died when you were a young atheist.

The Academy of Motion Make-Believe

We are movie stars, and you love us! You love the Oscars, the Academy of Motion Picture Arts and Sciences. Sciences? We are so talented. We are experts at realistic facial expressions. We deserve $10 to $20 million a year, a thousand times what a school teacher makes for teaching kids the basics of reading and writing.

Kodak Theatre. Dolby Theatre. (Insert brand here.)

I'd like to thank the Academy for giving me the opportunity to wear clothes more expensive than most people's cars. I'd like to thank my fellow thespians for this honor. They were all a pleasure to work with. Everyone is wonderful. We are always smiling.

Commercial break: BUY THIS SODA! BUY THIS CAR! BUY THIS HAMBURGER! James Bond sells Chryslers!

We have all advanced so much. A thousand years ago, entertainers would juggle and play instruments in front of the king, maybe put on a play for the village. Now, entertainers *are* the royalty. Each person who spends ten dollars at a movie theater keeps us in business. Ten dollars per DVD, fifteen dollars a month per cable channel. This keeps the racket going. Don't divert that money toward your local public school.

Oh, but we movie stars *hate* paparazzi. Why can't they just leave us nice people alone? Oh, but who buys *Star*, *Entertainment Weekly*? You do, the regular people, the peasants. Your obsession with who's dating whom keeps those photographers in business.

You shop at JCPenney while we wear Giorgio Armani, Gianni Versace, Jimmy Choo, Oscar de la Renta, Christian Louboutin, Alexander McQueen, Louis Vuitton, Vera Wang, and Christian Dior. Whom do you wear? Where do you summer? "The stars are dressed to the nines." What does that mean?

I want to thank my partners in crime: Warner Bros., DreamWorks, 20th Century Fox, MGM, United Artists, Universal, Paramount, Columbia, Tristar, Sony, Disney, Joseph Goebbels, Edward Bernays, and the propaganda machine.

"How about you? You have a 'berg' at the end of your name. Are you Jewish? Catholic . . . Wrong answer. Don't you want to work in this town? I would like to donate money to Israel and continue to work in Hollywood forever, thank you."

—Ted, the teddy bear (actual quote at Oscar ceremony)

Don't watch us in high definition. It shows our flaws. Vanity is not fair.

A-listers. We can get into nightclubs! People pay extra to get a table next to us. Want a table next to Leonardo DiCaprio? Forty grand. You got that Saudi oil money?

Don't play *Jaws* music to get me off the stage. I'm talking here!

Everything shines and shimmers. Jewelry comes with security guards. Harry Winston, Jacob the Jeweler. Forevermark.

Diamonds. So beautiful. Where do they come from? Trees? *Django* is a movie about slavery. Diamonds are slavery.

Argo is *such* a good movie. The word *good* is the extent of my nontrenchant vocabulary. I know you gave me that audiobook *Our Man in Tehran*, that real book *All the Shah's Men*, and that documentary on the 1979 Iran hostage thing. But I didn't watch any of 'em. But I was one of the first to see *Argo* for sure. There was such a buzz about it. Everybody was talking about it. *Good Morning America*, even the *NBC Nightly News*.

That bin Laden movie made it official. CIA-sponsored movies. They've come a long way since buying the rights to George Orwell's *Animal Farm* in 1955. Communists bad. Capitalists good.

It's pronounced "jango"; the *D* is silent. That's so cool.

Brad Pitt selling cologne. He's so hot right now. Buy life insurance. Edward James Olmos says you should trust banks.

Fap, fap, fap all over your wide-screen LED.

Asians, Latinos? Not this year. Did you see the image of crosses seven times throughout the Oscars? In the background, during movie clips. But we're not religious.

Get an American Express card. But not the black Centurion Card. That's for people like us who spend *at least* three hundred grand a year.

Embedded reporters. "OMG, OMG! Gerard Butler is here!"

And $48,000 swag bags. The IRS wants some of that.

I love your hair! Drink more soda. Celebrate dead famous people.

OMG! OMG! OMG! George Clooney. Ben Affleck. So talented. So important!

I wasn't even going to do this movie, but if I didn't do it, Spielberg wouldn't make it. So I did it. Twenty million? OK, thanks. Tom Hanks really struggled with the elements when he made *Cast Away*. Twenty million? OK, thanks.

"This has been an exciting year for movies," Michelle Obama said. "We can reach our dreams." Just keeping watching movies.

The red carpet has the blood of the poor on it.

Shape-shifting reptilians?

I know you agree with me. But this is not about you. You totally understand. Go back to your television. Stay entertained. Stay distracted. Stay sedated.

Hollywood is holy. Hollywood is holey. Holeywood.

Stop worshiping celebrities. Be your own celebrity.

Portlandia (Excerpts from the Show)

Portland is where young people go to retire.

The dream of the '90s is alive in Portland: the 1890s.

Portland is where you can put a bird on something and call it art.

You're in a technology loop.

Tucker Max protest organizing.

Keep Portland weird.

I'm gonna work on my core.

Cacao!

After you pay for it, it is free.

Mayor openly reggae.

All the hot girls wear glasses.

Pad thai is the perfect storm of allergies.

Lightning in a Bottle

Picture a cluster of electrons—a cloud, even—swarming around the nucleus of an atom, bound by gravitation and a little bit of love. Why not?

Picture this atom inside a red blood cell—not a permanent resident, just a traveler. A gypsy.

Picture the red blood cell traveling along a congested highway of other red blood cells, smaller platelets, cellular debris, and white blood cells in the carpool lane.

Picture this northbound traffic on Interstate Vena Cava all heading downtown.

Picture this atom again, feeling neglected, feeling small and unimportant in this downtown traffic at the Heart.

Picture this atom leaving the red blood cell, frustrated.

Picture this atom saying: "I have a name! I am Oxygen!"

Picture this atom finding friends—being paired up, even—O_2, in a large suburb near downtown known as the Lungs.

Picture this Oxygen, a molecule now, traveling the outer tributaries of the known universe, otherwise known as the Body, while on vacation, visiting the small intestines, the exotic Pancreas, the planned twin communities of the Kidneys.

Picture this Oxygen raising its own cloud of electrons over the "years" (the life span of a red blood cell is 115 days).

Picture this molecule growing old, settling down in the Lungs and pairing up with a retirement manager known as Carbon.

Picture this Oxygen molecule legally changing its name to Carbon Dioxide, CO_2, being propelled out of the comfortable Lungs with great turmoil, as the Body blows it out with a deep breath.

Ommmmmmmmmmmmmmmmmmm.

Ulysses

Just finished twenty-four hours of audiotape lectures on James Joyce's *Ulysses*. What an incredible masterpiece.

Yes, it's impossible to read and understand without help, but what groundbreaking concepts: one chapter is an entire play, complete with stage directions (150 pages); one chapter covers the entire span of the development of the English language from King James' Bible style through Shakespeare, to modern Irish slang, to gibberish; one chapter is a lady thinking in eight run-on sentences, with some of the sentences twenty pages long; in some chapters the narrator is the protagonist, in others it is a random dude in a bar, and in others it is minor characters; all of this while paralleling Homer's *Odyssey*.

This dude had his shit together.

Lightning in a Jail Cell

August 1, 2013, 10:18 a.m.

Sergeant: Good morning, everyone, and welcome to the Lightning in a Bottle tactical debriefing. As you read in the email I sent out last week, this is the first time this hippie-raver drug festival will take place here in Riverside County. We anticipate hundreds of arrests. The Southwest Detention Center near Temecula has been revamped to accommodate the load. Agent Smith, can you give us an update?

Agent Smith: Yes. Good morning, everyone. My undercover unit, otherwise known as the Special Investigations Bureau, working in conjunction with the Riverside County Sheriff's Department, is physically prepped for this festival. All my officers have shaved their mustaches and have grown about a week's worth of beard stubble. Unfortunately, we can't spare any of our officers deep undercover at Burning Man. Those are the guys with dreadlocks and long beards. You will be able to identify our two hundred men and women because they will have glow-stick necklaces.

Sergeant: Great work, Agent Smith. Now let's go get those brain-dead retards.

Several days later, after Lighting in a Bottle begins, Ilias, a twenty-five-year-old Russian American, is relaxing near the Temple of Consciousness after spending the last two hours helping a couple of weird-but-fun hitchhikers into town for some LIB paperwork. He's been well fed and is thinking about his girlfriend. He lights up a spliff.

A stubble-bearded guy in his late twenties with crew-cut hair and a brand-new tie-dye T-shirt and a glow-stick necklace sings the line "Excuse me while I light my spliff" as he sits down next to Ilias and then says, "What's up, bro?"

"Just chillin', man. What a great day. I got my girlfriend back. What a great start to this festival. So you like Bob Marley?"

"Oh hell yeah, bro. *Legend* is, like, my favorite album."

"*Legend*? Funny, you should check out some of the albums he made before he died. *Exodus, Survival, Uprising . . . Legend* is more like a posthumous 'best of' album."

"Cool story, bro. My name's Ponch." He offers a hand.

"I'm Ilias." Ilias gets up and tries to hug him.

"Whoa, whoa . . . easy, guy." Ponch waves him off. "I'm not a queer."

"What? Oh . . . it's not like that. See, at Burning Man, we all hug when we meet someone."

"Ah. Well, how 'bout a handshake for now?" Ponch extends his hand again. They shake.

"It's all good."

"So, Ilias, you know where I can find molly?"

"My girl probably has some. I'll be meeting up with her later."

"What are you smoking there? Marijuana?"

Ilias laughs and coughs a little on the joint. "Now you're on to something."

"I'll give you twenty bucks for it." Ponch tosses a bill at him.

"What the . . . nah, man. It's all goo—" Ilias is interrupted as Ponch quickly stands up and flashes a badge from under his shirt.

"DEA. You're under arrest!" Ponch yells as a few other men in Ilias's peripheral view come running over.

Ilias gets up and starts running. Within a few seconds, these thoughts run through his head: "What the fuck! What the fuck! Cops? I haven't done anything! I haven't done anything! There aren't cops at LIB. Run! Run! Maybe they're trying to rob me. Maybe they're with that dude Krash, who was hitting on my girl earlier and got pissed when I stood up for her. Shit, they're everywhere."

Ponch chases Ilias across the Temple grass while a few dozen people on yoga mats listen to a Peruvian pan-flute player onstage. One of Ponch's associates, a former college football player and former US Marine, tackles Ilias head on. An audible bone snap is heard by the spectators.

One of the yoga guys runs over to help Ilias. "Hey! Hey! Break it up! Break it up," he yells as he flails his arms.

Another of Ponch's associates stands in the way and also pulls out a badge. "Police business. DEA. Step back."

While Ilias lies on his belly, several of the men land their knees and shins on his back and side. "Stop resisting!" one of them yells as he jerks his wrists up into handcuffs and lifts him up to his feet by the wrists.

The men quickly start walking Ilias away. The rest of the yoga music audience just sits there stunned, immobile.

Someone yells, "Fuck the police!"

The men don't even respond. They walk Ilias out of view.

Later, back at the main stage, a remote-controlled helicopter with an HD camera buzzes over the crowd.

"Dude, check it out! That's so cool!" some guy says in the middle of the crowd, dancing away to a killer set by the Black 22's.

The helicopter takes facial-recognition recordings of everyone who looks up at it, then ascends away from the main stage and into the air. Becoming just a speck in the chemtrail-marred but otherwise blue sky, it heads back toward the Temple, passing it and entering the police command center. Inside a DEA RV, the pilot of the remote-control helicopter brings it down perfectly on top of the RV.

Ilias sits with a group of other arrested festival-goers in the hot sun, deep within the police encampment. He watches the RC helicopter land on the RV. "That's odd," he thinks.

No one explains anything to him or any of the other detainees. Finally, he is carted into the back of a police car while others are packed into a paddy wagon and taken for a twenty-minute ride to the Southwest Detention Center in the nearby town of Menifee, population ninety thousand.

Using his cell phone, he records the conversation he has with the police officer who drives him to Menifee.

Ilias: Officer, may I have permission to ask a question?
Cop: Sure.

Ilias: Why am I being separated from the others?

Cop: Lucky for you, I have to head back to central booking, and I wanted one perp to interrog—I mean, one citizen to interview on the way there.

Ilias: Lucky me.

Cop: I'm on your side, actually. I'm Internal Affairs, and I'm here to make sure the Riverside County Sheriff's Department respects the rights of the partygoers.

Ilias: You gotta be kidding me. I think I have a broken rib, and my wrists hurt.

Cop: Resisting arrest will do that to you. How long have you been dealing ecstasy?

Ilias: What? A pack of DEA undercovers beat me up Rodney King style because I was smoking a joint. I mean, allegedly smoking a joint.

Cop: You sure about that?

Ilias is quiet for a few minutes, then recovers.

Ilias: So do you know why it's called Lightning in a Bottle? It's like capturing something impossible, something rare. Something special. Now, it's just Lighting in a Jail Cell.

Cop: So we should just let you guys run around selling and doing illegal drugs?

Ilias: Why are drugs illegal in the first place? Alcohol was illegal in the 1920s, and look what a disaster that was. Organized crime was at its height. Al Capone was machine-gunning down people in Chicago. Surprisingly, it all went away when it was legalized. Same shit now with marijuana and cocaine.

Cop: You're a pretty smart kid. You a law student?

Ilias: Nah. I just read books. I've also read that you guys make money off all this drug trade. The prison industrial complex. Everyone from police to prisons need illegal drugs to keep you guys employed.

Cop: That might be true, but there will always be good guys and bad guys. And here we are.

They pull into the parking lot of the Southwest Detention Center. A couple of officers come over to take Ilias away. One yells over to the cop who was driving Ilias.

"Yo, Pac Man, whadda we got here?"

"This kid just confessed to me about selling ecstasy. And he was slamming himself around there in the back seat, in case you find any injuries."

The other officer laughs. "Yeah, a bunch of them doing that. So mysterious."

Ilias is shocked, dumbfounded. Silent. Holding his cell phone still recording in his pocket.

Several days after the festival . . .

Sergeant: Good morning, everyone. Let's begin. Let me first congratulate Agent Smith on a job well done. We've had about a hundred arrests. Some we'll have to throw back, but many will stick. I want everyone to dot their i's and cross their t's because the hippies have got a couple of do-good lawyers trying to defend them. All in all, we are winning the war against drugs, and I can't wait for Lightning in a Bottle next year. Dismissed.

The Lightning in a Bottle Festival was never held in Riverside County again.

Walls (An Adventure in Germany)

"i'm going to Germany!" i yell into my sister's face.

"I know," she calmly retorts. "That's why I bought you this book."

That's more or less the meat of the conversation i had with my sister a few weeks ago as i began preparing for a clubber's paradise of a vacation in Berlin. The book, *The Year That Changed the World*, reviews the events of 1989, the year the Soviet Union's twenty-eight-year-old wall around the Eastern Bloc countries "fell." No, it had nothing to do with Reagan's speech in Berlin two years earlier, where he said, "Mr. Gorbachev, tear down this wall." It had more to do with a series of midlevel German miscommunications and Gorbachev's restraint in not enforcing the iron curtain.

Did the Soviet empire really "fall"? Is the Cold War really over? Don't the Russians still have their government and all of their nukes? So a few smaller Eastern European countries jumped ship from communism to capitalism in 1989, followed by the Soviets themselves in 1991. So what?

i guess the world is a better place now. But what about the new walls that have gone up? Gorbachev is still alive today. What if he said, "Mr. Trump, tear down that wall" while looking at Mexico and Israel? People who support putting up walls have always been on the wrong side of history.

The Russians exploited their people and had to build an iron curtain to keep everyone in. Americans exploited the rest of the world and had to build an ironic curtain to keep everyone out.

Man, i haven't even gotten on the plane yet, and i feel all political and shit.

Berlin

Ladies and gentlemen! Welcome to German three-card monte. There are three rooms and one naked pope. Will he be in your room when you get to the hotel?

Well, before Captain Dufenschmurf and i can jump into that roundtable discussion, we find ourselves with our first wall of this adventure. Berlin just plopped us right out onto the street outside the airport, sans luggage. One minute we're on the plane. The next, we're deboarding and outside. No security, no nothing. Fucking Germans. So now we get to enjoy the adventure of finding our luggage. Then a cab. "*Verstehen Sie Englisch?*" Then find the hotel. Then pray to the devil that there is not a naked pope in our room.

First night out. We find a club called Suicide Circus in East Berlin. Vague memory of going literally underground.

Breakfast at Eurostars Hotel afterward. All the proper bourgeois shocked as the four of us sit down for a buffet—Captain Dufenschmurf, the Filipino Catholic from Long Beach; the pope, the Jewish Italian from Miami; Arby's, the Arab Muslim from Doha; and DJ Ass Maggots, the Satanist from Uranus. This dude we never met from Perth, Australia, Mick Roberts, whom we had met on Facebook in some secret group called the Council (i've said too much), canceled at the last minute. Something about having to go to jail.

"We need a bunch of towels for the room. There's blood everywhere."

Sleep all day. Next night. Tresor. Broken bottles everywhere. No one cleaning it up. Pope gets shard in arm.

Deep underground, within the vestibular labyrinthian stone walls, pulsates forth rhythm. Tribalism, and on the seventh note the devil said, "Let there be bass. And it was gooooooOD. OD."

Like the fires of Mordor, but this is no fiction. The darkest abscesses of Berlin with time make their way to the light. Sunlight's disinfection. "Nazi" and "love" are both dirty four-letter words here.

We have brought the pope back to his natural home: Berlin minimal techno.

Ich bin ein Berliner.

Diggin' our elbows into the chest of this cave where the first utterance of sound began. Hellooooo. Echoooo . . .

No time to write now right now. Save it for later.

Später

Ja, Ja. Much later.

Viel später.

That's what they all say. But then family gets in the way. Then pets. Then school. Then the career. Then the blood transfusion. Or whatever . . .

Boom boom boom. Hisssss. Steam released from the pirates of the Spree River. Engines grinding, BOOM BOOM BOOM BOOM. Sounds of cauldrons bubbling . . .

Tympanic membrane, malleus, incus, stapes, cochlea, labyrinth, semicircular canals, vestibule. My ears destroyed.

The subtleties of German words are important.

For example, if a girl says *nein*, that means "no." But if she says *neun*, that means "nine," which might mean nine inches or nine times. Or nine friends.

Booo. Bah. Unst unst unst. And *unt unt unt* . . . Bass in your face.

Third night. The long-awaited Berghain experience. We Google the club and realize it has a serious rejection policy at the door, like it's a game. None of the locals we talk to have ever been inside, including some stunning specimens of the female variety.

"You must look cool and different. Try not to speak or act drunk," one of the local girls advises us.

Because i've been to Burning Man five times, i take the leadership position on this one. i put on a white kimono with black lettering, some black Harajuku stacked boots, and a red-leather, zippered, bondage-style sex-play face mask. i dress the other guys in simple red cowboy masks and devil horns and lead them to the party on leashes. Everyone in front of the club checks us out as we arrive. Some even take pictures. The bratwurst guy outside the club yells over that we get free food after the party. In front of us in the Disney-style maze line, two Americans dressed like Nirvana peer jealously at us, then whisper to themselves.

"Oh my gOD, Tyler, look at those guys. There's no way *we're* getting in."

A group of chubby Spanish lesbians with tacky bright leggings gets rejected.

"Fuck Berghain! *Chupa mi verga!*" one of them drunkenly yells while having to do the walk of shame past everyone in line.

The Kurt Cobain/Courtney Love American couple in front of us gets in easily.

The group of bouncers and doormen saw us from the beginning of the line maze. They discussed our fate way before we meet them face to masked face. We don't say a word.

The smallest, gayest of the doormen nonchalantly wags his finger slowly from side to side and simply says, "No. Please go." But his eyes say, *You guys are trying too hard. Too Mickey Mouse. This is not Halloveen. You're not even vearing flannel or smoking cigarettes. Note to self—must buy kimono and masks for sex party at the Kit Kat Klub next veek.*

"Too much?" is my only reply. We walk away proudly.

"Our grandfathers died to come here and kick your ass! Is that it? Wait, maybe *his* grandfather. Nope, not mine, that guy over there," we all think in turn.

We go to Watergate instead. Rejected again. Something about already too many guys at the club, as they let in six underage dudes in skinny jeans, fedoras, and thick black glasses immediately behind us.

It's 8:00 a.m. Captain Dufenschmurf and Arby's have had enough. They take a cab back to the hotel. The pope and i Google an all-day "open-air" party.

We hail a cab, but when the driver sees the pope, now wearing my kimono like a huge Arab head scarf that nearly drags on the ground, he bails.

After toning down all our shit, we finally catch a cab.

Shit catapult.

Kosmonaut open-air day party. We meet this German teen, wanna-be American gangsta rapper named Evo.

"Hey, my man. Vhere you from? LA? Sheeet. Naughty by Nature. Das FX. My man. I'm a gangsta. Bitch, I might be." Evo really deserves more lines, but it's all kinda blurry . . .

There's always another room.

Berlin jail has great Wi-Fi.

Pope tells us about Portuguese breakfast outside Eurostars Hotel while squatting. People looking.

Random yellow pill found in taxi.

Solar bar. Past jellyfish. Rocket elevator. Stresemannstraße 76.

"If I had known they do anal, I would have come along for the ride."

"This one time in Doha . . ." Our pal Arby's chirps out another anecdote.

Michelberger Hotel Gangsta Rap

I'm the Kosher Kaiser.

Uh uh. Haben Sie Geld? Viel Geld.

Michelberger lobby,

East germanobobby bobby,

Trouble will find me,

Like a 69-gauge shotty.

French girls textin, Pierre about my body.

This girl rolling up weeeed in a cigarette.
Let's go up to my room for a bubble bath.
Wanna muzzle my face in your hairy armpit?
ScheiBe ScheiBe gib mir drei euro
And let's make big party party.
Hallo. Wie geht's?
Es geht mir gut
The ipope is drinking "Lift."
How is it?
"Piss in a bottle."
Seiche-cider
I need a syringe.

Berlin is kind of conservative when it comes to men with hair coloring. Pope and i had red hair accents. It's the Chicago of Europe.

In Schwarzenegger voice: "Is Berlin in tha hoooouse?"
Suicide Circus flyer found in my pants:

Programm Mai 2013
All You Can Beat Record Release Party
Housemeister
Microtrauma
MRI
PLASTIQUE
SUICIDE TECHNO PARTY
The Bugs

Artemis all-inclusive adult entertainment:
Workout,

Shower,

Dinner,

Dancing,

[REDACTED] with young German ladies for money?

Captain Dufenschmurf discussing euro discount with one blonde while [REDACTED REDACTED REDACTED] the other.

Shower,

pool,

Jacuzzi,

massage

Souvenir shopping

Doner kebap,

Vanille geschmack does a body good.

Got geschmack?

Currywurst mit pommes

I'm the Kosher Kaiser

Droppin' acid in your hefeweizen

Meanwhile, Tuesday nights.

Hipsters. Berlin.

Illusions: Vote for Shittybank or Douche Bank.

An Austrian girl asks me if there is any place in America like Berlin. i answer Silver Lake (insert the hipster neighborhood in your town here).

Berlin is also like San Francisco, but more gay.

Pope offers E150 for Alex to offer tall blonde some Popewurst and his schnitzel.

Anton, the tall Russian, shows the pope various death blows (please see pics). (There are no pics.)

"I want to like you, but you're not so polite."

Smoking is cool. Always smoke when at the front of the line.

Tattoos are cool. *Übercool.* Skinny jeans. Flannel. Thick black-rimmed glasses. Ma-te.

German girls are in a permanent bad mood. It's a cultural thing . . . pre-Hitler.

The hat is a proven prop in any club scene, but in Berlin, it is used pseudo-novelly. Wearing it backward is just lame. Wearing it slightly to the side is no longer cool (probably only in the last year or so, whereas in the States, it went out of style twenty years ago). Wearing it low, nearly covering the eyes (which is currently cool in the States), is not cool because it is too new and would be considered weird. So the only cool way to wear a hat is forward with the bill flipped up, which i like to call "nerdy white boy from the 1980s."

Saying *"entschuldigen Sie"* (excuse me) stopped the dad freakin'. Alex's dad. Who's Alex? Little Alex, the tall, skinny German teenager and his fellow droog John, the Colombian black dude with a hat, who invited us from the liquor store onto a bus, then to his apartment with his dad, who had just kicked him out. Well, we went back in. When i spoke in German, the dad answered "no problemo" and made sure the fat tabby cat with the gooey eyes (bilateral conjunctivitis) didn't attack us.

Später, viel später . . .

Getting into Chalet lounge: It's me (Ass Maggots), the pope, and our German hosts, Alex and John. Alex feels my shirt is too flashy (black-and-white patterned long-sleeved button-up with collar, one of my favorites and very rare, i might add), so he makes me wear his old, beat-up leatherish (pleather?) hipster jacket, which is too small for me, which makes it just right for the hipster look. Alex and i go up to the door first. German convo, something about being on the list, but i have to pay five euros. The bouncer says he likes my jeans (Shrine store, Melrose, blue-patterned goth). The pope and John were rejected. Racists! Anti-Semites! Pope wheeled and dealed, American style, until the bouncer let them in out of exhaustion.

Später, viel später . . .

Playing piano in a back room at Chalet. First guy beautifully fingers some B-minor chord progressions. Older guy waiting. This is gonna be good. Steps up. Has absolutely no idea how to play a piano. i politely leave.

A motley crew of people we meet inside: Nicolas Jaar. DJ Theo. "Teo." Like Theo Huxtable? Tough-looking bearded German dude with cute little pigtails. Tight jean shorts. Rolled-up sleeves.

We leave at 9:00 a.m.

Later, during the day . . .

Techno Viking is finally found panhandling under a train station. Good with directions. He is very nice . . . missing some teeth since his world-famous video. (You must YouTube "Techno Viking" at this point. Open a browser window. Go ahead. i'll wait.)

The Big Lebowski twenty-four hours a day on the hotel room TV.

Seventeen-year-old girls dancing to Don Omar, "*La mano arriba, Cintura sola.*"

Berlin Hauptbahnhof station.

Second attempt at Berghain, rejected. We would have gotten in if we were in a butt-fucking centipede line.

Bartender at 9:00 a.m.: "Facebook is sooo over."

Ads with Beyoncé selling bikinis for H&M everywhere.

The stoplights go red, then yellow, then green. It's all about timing.

The next wall to fall is Wall Street.

Berlin wall goes down. Berghain wall goes up.

Massage: Hans and Franz,

Dieter and Jieter

Special massage

"Vood u like the special happy bratwurst, or maybe a little schnitzel? Or both? Vee call that the German front and back."

Parov Stelar, Austrian electroswing.

There he is again, that crazy bum outside the Michelberger Hotel, yelling seemingly nonsensical phrases like "End the Fed," *"Banken sind ein Betrug"* (banks are a scam), *"Geld ist nicht real"* (money is not real), *"geben Sie nicht an, um Sparmaßnahmen"* (don't give in to austerity measures) . . . totally crazy . . . or . . . not?

München

High society at the Charles Hotel

Pope: "There is no chance an Oriental, a Jew, and a *you* are *ever* getting into Berghain."

Maggots: "What's a 'you'?"

Pope: "Whatever *you* are. An LA Persian red-haired space alien, shamblot, ra ra . . ."

Taxi runaround. Hotel turned out to be right next to the train station.

Ferrari F12berlinetta. Half Italian, half Saudi, with little red riding hood. Oof. Arabs feel safe in Munich.

FuckUALL store.

"Hey, be careful with that belt. It's E120."

"It's OK—we're DJs. We'll be opening for Blawan tonight at Harry Klein. Perhaps you've heard of me: DJ Ass Maggots?"

"Oh, really? I'm so sorry. I thought you guys were football hooligans. And who's that oriental?"

"Captain Dufenschmurf? He's our security."

We go to the Harry Klein club to see Blawan at 11:00 p.m. We get in easily. The crowd packs in over the next hour or so.

Random smiling young German approaches—Daniel the BuyBull thumper: "What religion are you?"

Maggots: "Well, you're not gonna like it."

"Lemme guess, Muslim."

"No, no. Not that bad. Satanic. Church of Satan by Anton LaVey."

We thought we ditched Daniel, but he resurrected every three tracks.

Ultra-lounges are out. Über-lounges are in.

i imagine having a conversation with an American bouncer about the need to keep the aisles clear, flash the lights at people blocking exits, enforce last call.

"It's about safety," he might say. Nah. It's about control. Liability. There is none of that here. No one clearing the aisles, no last call, no fucking rules. Everyone just seems to respect each other. If i wanted to, i could walk right up behind the DJ and pour a drink on all the equipment. But i don't. i don't need to or want to. Something about the walls being gone makes me not need to rebel.

My speech to the pope and Captain Dufenschmurf: Men. Your whole life you have waited for action. Your whole life you have sat behind desks, watched TV, read books, complained about philosophy. Always waiting for that magical day when you could accomplish something important, like Normandy beach, like climbing Mount Everest, like winning a hot-dog-eating contest. Men. Today is that day! We are going down these *goddamn* stairs in an offensive triangle football formation, and our directive is to get right in front of the DJ booth so that when that twenty-five-year-old DJ Blawan comes on, he'll see us, and he'll know. He will know . . . that we mean business. Let no one get in our way. No distractions. Ready. Set. Break.

Kick drum tattoo on Blawan's fingers.

"Why are they hiding bodies under my garage?"

Hieroglyphics on the walls of the club. Winged serpents eating people and shitting out beautiful silver eggs.

Who tries to write a story in the middle of the dance floor? I'M WRITING A STORY IN THE MIDDLE OF THE DANCE FLOOR!

There's Dieter from Sprockets¡ Dressed all in black with black pointy shoes and slicked-back blond hair.

Couple of dudes in clubby lederhosen. Curly mustaches.

Who let those Berliners in here with their flannel hipster grunge clothes¿ This is Munich¡

Postgame Analysis

We went home on a Monday. That Monday was thirty-two hours long (regular Monday is twenty-four hours, plus eight additional hours gained by flying from Europe to LA, catching the sun). Political walls, social walls, musical walls, communications walls, legal walls, financial walls, and velvet ropes. Sleep.

Gute Nacht and *auf Wiedersehen*.

Auf Wiedersehen, Au Lac Restaurant

Dear Au Lac Restaurant,

It has been a wonderful one-year relationship, but like all my relationships, it is now time for it to come to a tragic end.

It's not you; it's me. The open mic Monday Night DeLight has been a wonderful experience. Sean, Gianni, Chef Ito, Taylor, Rachel, and all the support staff have put together a unique space where anyone can perform anything in a loving environment.

Those Monday nights, which i went to almost every week for the last year, have rescued me from the depths of bleakness that my career has become. This last year has probably been the most stressful year, with the loss of my dear friend and colleague Dr. Karaalp, and the increasing presence of hospital politics, as the very foundation of my hospitalist work is at stake.

i *needed* Au Lac more than it needed me. And that's never healthy. i've never really been a stage performer, and it took me a while to conquer the anxiety and begin to have some fun with the reworkings of the writings of my upcoming fifth book. It became a drug.

This particular Monday night (last night) was particularly special for me, as i was performing the final part of my crazy four-part story about my trip to Germany in 2013. Usually Mondays are hectic because i am often on call Sunday night and have to deal with a landslide of new patients on Monday. But this Monday i happened to be off, giving me a chance to actually start practicing my piece Sunday night. i had to learn several German sentences and part of a Reggaeton song by Don Omar. The Germany piece is a metaphor for all the walls between us, whether borders of countries, nightclubs, sexuality, or social class.

i woke up Monday morning with my entire day planned around getting to Au Lac at 7:00 p.m. sharp, as that was the exact moment when parking opened up and the sign-in sheet started to fill up. J Brave and i raced through red lights on wild downtown streets in the Lamborghini while discussing music, film, life . . .

i made the mistake of talking to people and socializing upon entry into Au Lac, instead of beelining to the sign-up sheet as the comics do. By the time i realized my mistake, eighteen spots were taken.

Nineteen was not my lucky number; i did not get the nod to go up. i think part of it may have also been due to the "madness" of my style: drug and prostitution referencing and general debauchery à la Hunter S. Thompson and William S. Burroughs. Surely an animal-rights song or a poem about goddesses would have been better at an enlightened, plant-based restaurant. But that's not me. i blame no one but myself. My shit is mediocre at best. Not even my mom cares for it. My mom!

And so not going up to perform destroyed me. And i now welcome a new level of darkness that will swallow the sun, a bleakness that will make death metal sound like nursery rhymes.

If you are not one who performs an art, then maybe this whole rant will seem like total nonsense. But believe me, it is more important than fucking anything. This art—writing, performing, or otherwise—is all that matters. It is all that will be left when our useless bodies dissolve back into this mud-ball planet Earth.

And so you will never see me again at Au Lac. i love you all, peace out, and *Auf Wiedersehen*!

"It might be better to light a candle than curse the darkness, but turn that fucking light off. i'm trying to sleep."

—DJ Ass Maggots, May 1, 2018

Third Eye for Sale

Hi, sweetheart!

How are you?

Brilliant, I hope.

I know there is a lot of crazy going on right now, and resources are going to help our friends and families in dire need, as they should. I will be doing some donating myself.

I don't know if you have seen my Facebook posts, but I have been on an exciting journey of next-level awakening of late, especially over the last few weeks, that I must continue.

Recently, I have been initiated into four different third-eye powers by Paramahamsa Nithyananda, and I have been moving coconuts with my third eye and doing third-eye readings, body scanning, and healing for others! It's incredible!

I am new at the body scanning and healing, but the power is getting stronger with practice.

I'm currently fundraising to get to India for Superhuman training next week, and I need all the help I can get today.

Here is the link to my GoFundMe campaign!

It officially ended yesterday, and I am continuing to fundraise through PayPal, Venmo, QuickPay . . .

I'm just beyond one-fifth of the way there. Only $12,500 left to raise!

Easy, right!

I depart Wednesday, the thirteenth, and return on January 11. I am working to get all of the tuition paid today.

I would LOVE it if you would check out my campaign and donate through PayPal, Venmo, or QuickPay today.

Thanks so much!

No sleep till India!

Big hugs to you!

Sending lots of love and hugs.

I never thought I would ever be heading to India, but now I have the best possible reason to go. Be sure to read all the way to the end. There are some *lovely* art pieces being offered for sale by De Camille to support my mission, and check back in a day or so for more of her art to be added.

Wow! I just had the most intense and powerful healing through this latest healing instruction. If you have free time today, I would love to talk with you about all of this.

Tuesday, 9:35 a.m.

I wanted to share about this program in such a way that the tuition cost and the Eastern culture guru relationship isn't what's focused on. I want it to be understood just how important this truly once-in-a-lifetime opportunity is to me and the incredible impact my doing this program will have on your life, on the ones you love, your family members, your friends, your neighbors, anyone and everyone who has a health issue, a wealth issue, or any other blocks in their lives that are keeping them from living the inspiring and joyful lives that they truly desire.

I have been struggling with playing much smaller in life than what I have always known I am capable of, as many have. I have brilliant ideas, inspired ideas, but I have yet to be able to bring those ideas to life. When I return from India, I will finally be able to powerfully create them, and I will be empowered to help anyone who wants it with any issue in their lives. I will be able to see the root issue, the root patterns, and heal it, not just counsel them through it. I will be able to look at any situation in their lives and see the entire picture and the solution. This is how I will be empowered through the rest of the tuition being funded. If it is paying back of a loan that is desired, with everything I will be imbued with during this program, paying that back will not be a problem in the slightest.

Not doing the program is not an option for me.

Knowing the profound impact I can have right now on the lives of all the people we know who are physically ill or are in emotional pain, in self-hatred and self-denial patterns, are suffering from addiction, a lack of joy-inducing employment, debts, financial issues, I cannot miss this opportunity to help and let the people in our lives continue to suffer unnecessarily.

All of these lives can be impacted in the most beautiful ways right now and not at some undetermined, far-off date down the road or never.

There is still time to bring all of this healing and relief to the people in our lives right now. I can still pay the tuition today and be on my flight tomorrow. I received donations totaling $1,000 yesterday. So my remaining balance is $11,000.

This is not a dream for me, and this is not something that I really want to do. This is what I must do, why I chose to be born, to have *this* breakthrough in consciousness at *this* time, to have *this* level of loving and positive impact on others, to go *this* big, to be *this* empowered. Make no mistake, I am not being given money to do a yoga program in India. I am being empowered to deeply empower you, all of the people we know and beyond. What you will be receiving in turn is unfettered access to me, a next-level healer, third-eye counselor, and miracle worker upon my return.

Thank you so much for taking the time to read this, and I hope I have made it clear what is really at stake and what is available with your generous contribution through PayPal and directly to my bank account today, using the same email through QuickPay or Zelle through Chase.

With love,

[REDACTED], soon to be Superhuman. ☺

Saturday, 7:42 p.m.

Here's hoping on a wing and a prayer. Will you be my angel? I will be your weekly bodyworker, third-eye counselor, body scanner, next-level healer, if desired, remote visioner, and more!

I truly want someone to enjoy the one-of-a-kind offer I have made with these epic, next-level services for six to eighteen months. 😀

My angel on Earth needs to land tonight or tomorrow. My flight leaves Monday morning. 😊

Totally happy to have a phone chat tomorrow! I will tag you to my bodywork offer. 😀

Perhaps you may know someone who would enjoy this offering. 😊

(from a girl i met once in 2009)

Channel Surng

2 Broke Girls
Opening dialogue where two mildly attractive, slightly hallucinogenic-looking girls comment on cheap furniture they newly purchased. Audience laughs on cue. Cuts to commercial quickly.

American Ninja Warrior
Contestants leap through fantastic obstacles while enthusiastic announcers make it seem like this is important. The crowd looks like suburb zombies. Cuts quickly to commercial.

Breaking Pointe
Dramatic music backdrops people in theatrical costumes who seem to be competing in a reality show. "I think my thumb is broken," despairs one of the effeminate men. More accidents, then cuts to commercial.

Law and Order: Criminal Intent
A detective-type drama. Police question someone in his own house. Everyone is white. Bad acting. Looks like a murder happened. How exciting.

Mistresses

Police again doing a good job, helping a lost child. Then a couple, half-naked, fooling around in bed. A man with a *terribly* fake French accent seduces a woman, then says he is going back to France. This elicits a heated argument. Cuts to commercials.

Commercials: Mazda, Burger King, Macy's, Advil, Best Foods Mayonnaise, promo for *Trophy Wife* show, promo for *Eyewitness News Mornings*, Chevrolet, Farmers Insurance.

The show resumes four minutes later.

KCAL 9 News

Commercial break. Chevrolet again.

New Girl

Romantic drama. Indian bride is jilted as Indian man declares he loves an American girl in the crowd and wants to marry her in a Presbyterian church.

Law & Order: Special Victims Unit

More upstanding police doing a good job trying to solve crime.

Several more channels, all on commercials.
More detective shows on cable.

The Big Bang Theory

Apparently not about how the universe was created. Cuts to commercial.

Cops
Polite, well-spoken police arresting crazy white trash with guns and swords and missing teeth.

T. J. Hooker
Unfortunately on commercial break.

Rules of Engagement
Laugh tracks. Everyone speaks in turn.

SportsCenter
SportsNation
College football
ESPN
Angels Weekly
High school football
Laker Girls
Fox Sports Live

i put down the remote control, take out a gun, and shoot myself in the head.

Argo Fuck Yourself

i just finished watching Ben Affleck's directorial pièce de résistance *Argo*, and i am moved. First of all, i am so happy to contribute twenty dollars to the coffers of Sir Affleck. I hope he made enough money from this movie and won enough awards to keep the genius coming for another eon.

Disclaimer: i have also read the documentary account *Our Man in Tehran*, which came out, like, twenty years ago. i know most of you haven't read it, but no need to worry. The details of how the *actual* caper went down are terribly boring and totally different from the movie *Argo*, so i would just totally disregard that book, with all of its painstakingly accurate details. Also, that book had the nerve to make Canadian ambassador Ken Taylor and the Canadian embassy heroes and downplayed the role of the CIA. Our very own CIA! Can you believe that? i know the CIA got a bad rap in 1963 for killing JFK and in 1965 for killing Malcolm X and in 1968 for killing MLK and RFK, but they redeemed themselves in 1979 with their bold heroics and brilliant leadership in smuggling the six American ambassadors out of Iran. Three cheers to Ben Affleck for putting aside historical accuracy and making the CIA heroes once again! Who cares if the actual idea of a movie as a cover was chosen by the American ambassadors themselves from a list of three options?

Now let's talk about Ben Affleck's acting chops. i have heard some Debbie Downers state that they don't think Ben Affleck is a "good" actor. What the hell does that mean? Convincing? Maybe. Believable? Maybe. Versatile? Sure. Transcending the art of cinema? Of course. Ben Affleck is none of those things because he is something greater. He carries a certain stoical smugness all the time, as kind of a secret message between him and the audience that says, *Oh shit, I'm just a bumble-fuck Southie from Boston, and I have no idea why I'm famous. Thank you, Matt Damon!* Now name any other actor that can deliver such a specific secret message to all of his audience every time. That's acting!

Being Iranian, I can attest to the way Iran—or as i like to call it, *Persia* (doesn't sound so terroristy)—is depicted in this film. Yes, everyone there is scary. From the bearded men at the bazaar to the bearded men at the airport, to the bearded men in the rally, to the bearded women—i mean, women with hijabs—everyone *hates* Americans and Westerners in general. The movie nailed this point. i especially like the touch of a man hanged to his death from a construction crane just outside the Tehran airport. Those people are barbarians! i actually haven't been to Iran since I was one year old, but I watch *ABC World News Tonight*, so i know the real deal.

Finally, i would like to congratulate my fellow Iranians, including friends and relatives, who went out and contributed financially to the success of this movie. Sure, there were no Iranian heroes or even good guys in the movie. Sure, they didn't show any of the food, culture, or music of the region. But in all fairness, Mr. Affleck was stuck with only 120 minutes in his budget, and you know how much time those Iranian parties take to film. i commend those of you Iranians who said this was a "good" movie. That means you were entertained, and that's what matters. And that's what history will remember.

Cosmic Dancer

Look, i'm just here to dance.

i don't care about the guest list. i don't care about drink specials. i don't care about celebrities.

i'm just here to dance.

Give me a 2/4-time undulated bass march, synthetic groove, breaks, minimal techno.

i just want to dance.

i don't need to go to the bathroom. i don't need a cigarette break. i don't need a drink from the bar.

i'm just here to dance.

You might find me in the middle of the dance floor, spinning around with my eyes closed, smiling. i don't need to text anyone. i don't need to look for anyone. i'm not here to *meet* anyone.

i just want to dance!

i don't care what you're wearing. But if you have a unihorn, i won't mind. If you have a funny costume, i won't mind. If you look sexy, i won't mind.

But i'm here to dance.

i don't care who the DJ is. But if it's divaDanielle, i won't mind.

(This story was written in its entirety on the dance
floor of King King on Hollywood Boulevard
during a divaDanielle set in 2013.)

Facebook: Are You Cheating on Me?

Dear Facebook: Are you cheating on me?

Are you selling my information to third parties?

Are you working with the government?

Is this what "there's no such thing as a free lunch" means?

Facebook, i thought we had something special. You're like my diary. i write all my intimate thoughts inside you. i post pix. i tag friends. You said it was our little secret. But now i hear about people in court having Facebook evidence used against them. You little whore!

i'm not upgrading our dinners to Red Lobster anymore. From now on, it's only Sizzler. No more putting on the white gloves, listening to dubstep, and doing my light show. You don't deserve it.

Back in the day, when i was courting Myspace, my personal info was never violated like this. Sure, Tom's Myspace was kind of cheesy, and we all had fake names, but we had fun. We listened to music. We had zany, colorful walls. Facebook, you came across all classy, all upscale. But now look who's really cheap.

Anyway, you can't prove i did any of those things. i'll claim it as poetic license, fiction, or identity theft. i'll claim the pix were Photoshopped. As Scarface said, "I got such a good lawyer, that by tomorrow you'll be working in Alaska. So dress warm."

And by the way, i've been cheating on you too. i've been seeing Instagram, Snapchat, and Twitter. i know, i know. None of them are like you. You are like social crack. i used to love you, but now i'm just addicted to you.

Facebook, i will outlast you. i'll be around long after you're gone. i'm not sucking your metaphorical dick anymore.

Well, maybe a little more.

You Support Slavery

You abhor traditional African slavery, which cursed our civilization until the 1860s. You detest racism and the idea of keeping another human as chattel. You are a good person. You've read *Uncle Tom's Cabin*. You believe in treating people kindly. Well, whatever happened to those freed slaves?

As you may remember from your history classes, after the Civil War, many blacks migrated to the North, taking up the lowest-paying jobs available. Others stayed in the South, doing the same thing. For the next one hundred years, segregation continued, in the South officially, whereas in the North, economically. Where do you think the black ghettos in every big city came from? Our country didn't provide anything further than the right to leave the slave masters. No education, no instructions, no assistance to find long-lost family members, no forty acres, and no mule.

"How does any of this apply to me now in the twenty-first century?" you might ask. Well, what do you think of poor black people now? What do you think of the homeless? Where do you think gangs came from? Why are so many black men in prison?

Where do diamonds come from? Where does gold come from? Have you seen the conditions in African mines? Why are the countries of Africa still impoverished? Have you seen Shell's exploitation of the oil reserves in Nigeria? No? But have you seen Hollywood movies stereotyping Somali pirates but failing to show the foreign influences in keeping Somalia poor? i bet you have.

If you're still with me at this point, you're probably the wrong target audience. You probably do care and are involved. This message is for the person who stopped reading after the first paragraph. This message is for the person who doesn't realize there is actually more trafficking of humans for labor and sex around the world today than there was during the peak of the African slave trade. This message is for the person who is a debt slave, who gives four months of his or her salary to a government that clandestinely uses that money to kill people in destitute foreign lands.

But maybe you are the person i'm trying to reach. Let's transplant you back to the 1790s. Would you be against slavery then? Abolitionism wasn't popular then. i get the feeling you kind of go along with what is popular. You follow the law, right? Slavery was *legal*. You respect our Founding Fathers, right? They said "all men are created equal" while their slaves brought them their afternoon tea. i'm gonna guess that you would probably go along with slavery, just like you go along with owning a dog or a cat today, just like you buy gold and diamonds, just like you eat cows and chickens from factory farms, just like you feel that poor people are poor because they are lazy or stupid or passed up their opportunity or are drug addicts.

You believe in the free market. That's the same market that made a "big negro with good teeth and a strong back" fetch a higher price. *Free* market? Right.

So what is my point? Why have i wasted your valuable *free* time? i honestly believe that you support slavery. Sure, looking back on it now, 150 years later, you will continue to tell me that you don't. But would you be willing to break the law? Would you be willing to risk your family's lives? Your career? i think not. i think you would not "rock the boat" (pun intended). You might not have liked it, but you would have gone along with it. You would not want a revolution. You would not want to start trouble. This is not a historical piece. This is an essay for today. Egregious and horrific inhumanities continue all around us, many of which we are indirectly responsible for, as leaders of the *free* world. What are you going to do about it? It doesn't really matter because revolution is coming, with or without you.

OK, that's it. i'll stop talking into the mirror.

Surgical Strike

If actual surgeons were as inaccurate as military surgical strikes or "smart bombs," people would go in for an appendectomy and have their gallbladder taken out. They would go in for a cataract and come out with missing teeth. They would get admitted for an overnight knee replacement and end up staying for weeks in the ICU due to sepsis because the surgeon didn't wear gloves.

The only thing "surgical" about a military strike is that people are sure to be cut open, sure to spill blood, and sure to pay a heavy price.

The Rhyming Dictionary

Aaaah, bruh. Abracadabra. Ha, Jah, moi? Utah. Spa, Allah, blah-blah, bourgeois, Casbah, chamois, Chechnya, chutzpah, Edgar Degas, faux pas, foie gras? Lady Gaga? Hell nah . . . Grandpa and grandma's hoo-ha and hoopla, hurrah, oompah oompah. Quinoa, patois, viva Syrah, voilà! Opa! Ta-ta . . .

Aloha Abdullah and Adana! Allahu Akhbar and Admiral Akbar. Baklava, Bogotá, Chippewa, coup d'état, guarana, inshallah, Karbala, la-di-da, ma-and-pa, Mardi Gras, Ferrari Modena, moussaka. Omaha, Ottawa, Panama, polenta, tempura, Shangri-La.

Ayatollah je ne sais quoi, ménages à trois, petit bourgeois phenomena.

Black. Crack. Back to the click clack hacky sack. i'll smack that backpack on the Amtrak. Attack bareback like my ball sack on Balzac. The carjack is the blowback, comeback with Cognac. The drawback is cutbacks. Fast-track flapjack flashback, guaiac the poop in a hatchback, my jet-black hunchback. No Big Macs for a snack, Jack.

AU LAC!

George Orwell Quotes

"To say 'I accept' in an age like our own is to say you accept concentration camps, rubber truncheons, Hitler, Stalin, bombs, aeroplanes, tinned food, machine guns, putsches, purges, slogans, Bedaux belts, gas masks, submarines, spies, provocateurs, press censorship, secret prisons, aspirins, Hollywood films, and political murders."

"As I write, highly civilised human beings are flying overhead, trying to kill me.

"They are 'only doing their duty.' Most of them, I have no doubt, are kind-hearted law-abiding men who would never dream of committing murder in private life. On the other hand, if one of them succeeds in blowing me to pieces with a well-placed bomb, he will never sleep any the worse for it. He is serving his country, which has the power to absolve him from evil."

"There is no such thing as law, there is only power."

"From a very early age, perhaps the age of five or six, I knew that when I grew up I should be a writer. Between the ages of about seventeen and twenty-four I tried to abandon this idea, but I did so with the consciousness that I was outraging my true nature and that sooner or later I should have to settle down and write books."

Zombie America

"Yo, Huck, look at the surveillance camera. The zombies have encircled the building!"

"You're right about that, Tom. Jim and I just came in from the perimeter. They're everywhere."

"What are we gonna do? There's too many of them. And I can see more and more coming. I knew I shouldn't have come in to work today."

"Don't worry, Tom. We'll get through this. We just need to get organized. I think if we actually let them in a few at a time, we can probably handle them."

"Huck, did you see what happened in Newark? It was twenty degrees outside, but the zombies just piled up outside the store. All types—young, old, black, white, men, women. The people inside tried to let in a few, but it turned into chaos. The zombies could smell the opportunity and began to stampede. It didn't end well."

The four store employees continued to plan out their strategy. Tom Sawyer and his girlfriend, Becky; Huckleberry Finn and his African American friend, Jim. They armed themselves with walkie-talkies, flashlights, Tasers, caffeine.

The next twenty-four hours would be hell. Then it would be over.

"ATTENTION WALMART SHOPPERS! WELCOME TO THE DAY-AFTER-THANKSGIVING BLACK FRIDAY MEGA-SALE. BEGIN SHOPPING!"

Like the zombies of the movies that would groan "braaaa-ins" as they slithered toward you, these consumer robots also had a mantra: "Sale. Saaaale."

We Are All Superstars

Perish's Studio 69, fog, Skrillex, lights, Superstar DJ Keoki, drinks, Dave Navarro, DJ Slutz, more fog, Brooke, dancing girls, Schlauting Thomas, Erin Zealous Tha Kernal, Juliana, Nick, Jess O'Donnell, kids, girls making out, Donald Cassel, Jared, Eddie Izm, Ragz, Tony, Scarlett Snow, Nicole Passion Cruz, Tim Rich, Johnny Guerilla Republic, drinks, UV white light, Buffalo Bill, girls trapped in a well, naked dudes with wings, Goner and bunny ears, glow-fur, dubstep, house music, more fog, snacks in my pocket, feathers, tight abs, butts, bleeding tympanic membranes. Bathroom breaks. Water. More water. Freaks. Weirdos. Lasers. Boobs. Pasties. Cell phone photography. Big camera photography. Greasy mustache man photography. White Adidas tracksuits. Light shows. Face paint. Nipples. Tatou 333. Sipping balls. Sparks. Love. Banners. Techno. Mohawks. Stacks. Platform shoes. Glitter. LED lights. Goggles. Bleach. Boys on girls, boys on boys, girls on girls. Girls on boys. Pogo Pink Tie. Braids, Mickey Rourke, John Goodman *Big Lebowski* creepy sketchy. All-Star Variety Show, insert your name here.

Credit Union

As i wait in line for a teller, the all-powerful message-box television tells me what to believe. Ex-congresswoman Giffords issues a statement on the anniversary of her shooting urging Americans to curb gun violence. How paradoxical is it that with every mass shooting, there is a huge surge in gun sales as citizens prepare for possible new gun bans?

We always move like sheep. Sheeple. Even now, the big news pushed out by the talking heads in a box is the *fiscal cliff*. What a scary concept! Our economy is on the brink of going over the edge. Everybody needs to tighten up their checkbooks and work a little harder. Those of us who still have jobs, that is. The economy is broke! What does that even mean? Gibberish. We collectively already forgot about the great bank robbery of 2008.

Oh, you don't remember? Remember the great Wall Street crash of 1929? Remember the Glass–Steagall Act of 1933 that prohibited regular banks from interacting with investment banks? Probably not. Remember the repeal of the Glass–Steagall by a bipartisan congressional committee in 1999? Definitely not. They set us up. They fixed it for the investment banks. Again.

Dead. Should Be Dead.

John Belushi: Dead
John Candy: Dead
Dan Aykroyd: Should be dead
"James Brown Is Dead"
Justin Bieber: Should be dead
Liberace: Dead
Freddie Mercury: Dead
Barry Manilow: Should be dead
Neil Diamond: Should be dead
John Goodman: Should be dead
Jeff Bridges: Should be dead
Kurt Cobain: Dead
David Grohl: Should be dead
Emmanuel Lewis: Should be dead
Gary Coleman: Dead
Todd Bridges: Should be dead
Dana Plato: Dead
Michael Jackson: Dead
Madonna: Should be dead
Nazis: Dead
Blues: Dead

Dubstep: Dead
Trap: Should be dead
Disco: Dead
Muddy Waters: Dead
Kenny G: Should be dead
Elvis: Dead
Aretha Franklin: Dead
Queen Latifah: Should be dead
Ray Charles: Dead?
Stevie Wonder: Should be dead
Paul McCartney: Should be dead
Sam Kinison: Dead
Andrew Dice Clay: Should be dead
Rock 'n' roll: Dead
Television: Should be dead

New Year's 1913

"What is this new crazy music i'm hearing?" i say to the chap next to me.

"It's called 'swing.' It's the new thing."

"Hmphhh," i gruff. i don't want to be here. i don't want to be anywhere. i think i want to disappear. It's not that 1912 was a bad year. i did OK, made $666. It's just that i have nothing to look forward to. My boss at the bank said there's going to be a big change this year, something called the Federal Reserve. i dunno—it all sounds kind of depressing to me. i leave the main ballroom of the New Year's party and climb out on the fire escape. It's time to snuff it. i look at the ground ten floors down and jump. Some kind of flying vehicle with a "DMC" moniker on the front of it catches me.

i wake up in a big steel trash can looking up at the very place i just jumped from. Apparently uninjured, i brush myself off, wipe my flowing white beard, and climb to the ground, then back up the fire escape and into the party once again. i hear that same swing music, but this time with heavy, deep sonic vibrations penetrating my very chest, nay, my very soul. i see a strange-looking fellow with some kind of translucent necklace.

"Say there, old chap, is this music called 'swing'?"

"Electro-swing. Happy 2013, bro!" He then starts having some kind of standing seizure on the dance floor.

Wait, what's this? i see many others dressed like him all doing the same thing on the dance floor. Is this voluntary? Are they . . . dancing? What happened to the party? And why did this man call me his brother? After talking to a few of the patrons here, it seems that i have traveled one hundred years into the future. i no longer feel like committing suicide.

"Love your look, dude. That's so retro!"

"Love No Thotties" by Chief Keef (Re-white)

These ladies act like neighborhood prostitutes but yearn to be internationally famous
You have never seen $100,000? I have that amount in my suitcase
Would you like a drink? I know you are an alcoholic
And I know other African Americans are jealous of me
I'm currently driving my Ferrari while wearing Louis Vuitton loafers
Lady, my religion is Rastafarianism, although I carry a gun
I wish another black man would try to betray me
So I could get his blood on my $500 shoes
I wear $1,000 belts because I am a rich black man
I enjoy shooting other men with my 9mm handgun
Did I mention I have expensive shoes? Look at them!
I can afford to buy my lady friend a buttocks implant
I drink prescription-strength cough syrup containing codeine and promethazine,
and it makes walking difficult

I prefer it mixed with peach soda

You are friends with my enemy; I will shoot him in the mouth with my 9mm handgun

You were speaking with him on the phone while performing fellatio on me, and he was unaware!

I did not even try to

You want to become famous? My name is Keith Cozart, otherwise known as Chief Keef,

and I can help you

You are as classy as a $300 gold bottle of Armand de Brignac Ace of Spades champagne

The other ladies are reminiscent of a cheap ten-dollar bottle of pink Moscato

Ma'am, I am quite powerful. You can join me in this lifestyle

That is because I am quite fond of you

That is the only reason I use my phone to send you texts and live video chats

However, I only want to have sexual intercourse with you, not get married

But you must keep good oral hygiene and follow my directions

Original Lyrics

These bitches act local and think global

Never seen a hundred thousand, well let me show you

What you want to drink, I know you hate being sober

And I know all these niggas hate Chief Sosa

I'm cruising in my 'Rari with my Louie loafers

Bitch I'm a Rastafari, I'm a toolie toter
Wish a nigga would try to screw me over
Now I got blood on my Louie loafers
I wear $1,000 belts cause I'm a rich nigga
Nina like to bust a bitch the way she hit niggas
Shoes cost a bunch of shit, look at my kicks nigga
Could've bought a ass for my bitch nigga
I'm off this Actavis, it got me leanin' over
I poured up four of Purp in some peach soda
You friend of a opp, I'mma Nina blow him
You was on the phone with him, sucking my dick, he ain't
even know it
I ain't even try to
You wanna Glo up, baby Keef got you
You's a gold bottle, these hoes pink Moscato
Baby I'm the owner, you can be my castle
Baby 'cause I like you
Only reason I text you and why I Skype you
I just wanna fuck on you, I don't wanna wife you
But you gotta brush your teeth and do what I say, though

The Doctor Moshes

So the doc takes drug reps to Slayer instead of the usual Vegas shit as he goes back to his primal roots.

Visions of the pit: counterclockwise rotating swarm of mad, muscular men; blistering-tempo slugfest; grim shadows; and sweat—tattoos that pass in a flash as you get kicked in the head by a crowd swimmer. Robust bellies and grisly faces, incongruous shapes. You realize this is a bad time to be filming. Frenzy builds with triplet-marching metal chords. This is the apocalypse.

Propaganda death ensemble
Burial to be
Corpses rotting through the night
In blood-laced misery
Scorched earth the policy
The reason for the singe
The pendulum it shaves the blade
The strafing air blood raid

Tom Araya barks out lyrics as you circle the pit. There is no escape. A skinny girl with glasses punches you in the face. Where are *your* balls?

Now, you scream (no falsettos!) and start hopping up and down. This is your song. You are a giant now. Dark men (only one African American in the crowd, actually). Beards. Neck tattoos. Gang signs. Scars external and internal. You punch up and hit another crowd surfer. The circle loses order as the tempo reaches that magical number. It might as well be *Fahrenheit 451*. Now people are flying at you from all directions, and you realize *there are only targets and missiles in here.* You become a missile and project across the room in a rabid, elbow-dropping, grand mal seizure of dance emotion straight into the huge Samoan guy with a dozen names tatted on his chest. He grins, grabs you, and tosses you like an action figure up onto the flop.

You are horizontal now.

A squirming zombied parade of arms below you propels you toward the stage. You see the wonderful old-fashioned chandeliers of the Hollywood Palladium. The crowd moves you toward the speakers. A wall of Marshall stacks tidal waves sonic energy into your eardrum, then your malleus is hammered, your incus is anvilled, and your stapes is stirruped. Your auditory nerve shoots this forward to your temporal cortex brain matter while your inner ear remembers that you are still horizontal, floating above this Halloween spectacle. Hairs on the inner-ear mechanisms singed by the metal, the heavy metal. You see your own feet, and behind them is the ceiling. You are going down. People are now stepping on you.

Murder is my future, killing is my future,

Suffocation. Sweat. Meaty hands grab at you and lift. You are on your feet again! A large mustached Mexican with a missing front tooth grins, pats you on the back, then throws your ass back into the shark tank. Blood is everywhere: gashed lips, broken noses, edematous eyes, knees bent backward, and someone stopping to tie his shoes.

White men with shaved heads, white men with long hair, Latina cholas with black-rimmed glasses punching people, punching you! Someone with blue flannel and a blue bandana. Ca—rip . . . Forlorn Uncle Sam–looking men, wizards, trolls, hobgoblins, Spider-Men, and Peter Parkers. Rogues, ex-cons, Guitar Center employees, and gas station workers. Wild animals.

Splish, splosh. Skin on skin. Your face pressed flush against the hairy back flesh of another man. Everything in slow motion. Nooo!

"Yahhh! Slayyyer!"

Scatologic now, your soiled pants won't survive this.

Martyr to the kingdom of the dead. Infamous. Butcher. Angel of Death!

Mystic atavistic ritual, religious circle like Mecca. Banshee screams. Maybe we are a whirlpool of flesh. Jump in and be baptized, reincarnated. Bouncing breasts mother you around the pit. Soft landing. Calloused work hands pushing you along.

We spiral like galaxies.

This is that I-don't-give-a-fuck-about-anything type of mosh pit. This is that I-will-live-forever-and-literary-critics-can-suck-my-dick type of mosh pit. i see James Joyce, Henry Miller, George Orwell, Hunter S. Thompson, Charles Bukowski, Bret Easton Ellis, why not? i ride for all of my literary homies in this pit. i ride for metal.

We continue to circle in counterclockwise revolutions. And no one has health insurance.

"Get Low" by Lil Jon (Re-white)

Multiples of three, darn, you are attractive, continue to dance on the tip of my penis.

Let us dance near the ground,

To the window, to the wall

My testicles are perspiring,

Nice ladies crawling.

To all: ejaculate! ejaculate! good people! Everyone ejaculate, ejaculate! Golly

To all: ejaculate! ejaculate! good people! Everyone ejaculate, ejaculate! Golly

A short, cute, good-looking girl enacting a euphemism for getting inebriated on marijuana and alcohol and possibly crack cocaine. So nice, so nonmalodorous, will she have sexual relations with me?

I am quite preoccupied with this due to her beauty.

I have frequented this establishment for this sole purpose.

Can I snap your panty string with my fingers?

The club owner has alerted the security guard to my motives.

I am now intoxicated, and they are threatening to remove me from said premises.

She continues to get intoxicated on alcohol and possibly marijuana or cocaine.

I enjoy it when nude women shake their hips in an up-and-down bouncing motion, causing their buttocks to shake, wobble, and jiggle.

Prostitute, respect men from the city of Atlanta, Georgia.

Your vagina feels this way because the musical group Ying Yang Twins is here

I am known as Lil Jon, although my real name is Jonathan Smith,

and my cohorts are known as the East Side Boyz.

We all enjoy nude female buttocks and breasts.

Now come over here, lady, and impress me with your sexual gyrations.

If you are too classy to dance in a low squatting stance, do not bother getting up.

Original Lyrics
[Chorus:]

Three, six, nine, damn you're fine move it so you can sock it to me one mo time

Get low, Get low [six times]

To the window (to the window), to the wall (to the wall),

To the sweat drop down my balls (my balls)

To all these bitches crawl (crawl)

To all skeet skeet motherfucker (motherfucker!) all skeet skeet goddamn (goddamn)

To all skeet skeet motherfucker (motherfucker!) all skeet skeet goddamn (goddamn)

Shortie crunk so fresh so clean can she fuck that

Question been harassing me in the mind this bitch is fine

I done came to the club about fifty-eleven times now can I play with yo

panty line club owner said I need to calm down security guard go to sweating

Me now nigga drunk then a motherfucker threaten me now

She getting crunk in the club I mean she working

Then I like to see the female twerking taking the clothes off *buckey* naked

ATL. Ho don't disrespect it

Pa pop yo pussy like this 'cause Ying Yang Twins in this bitch

Lil Jon and the East Side Boyz wit me and we all like to see ass and titties

Now bring yo ass over here ho and let me see you get low if you want this Thug

Now take it to the floor (to the floor) and if yo ass wanta act you can keep yo ass where you at

Four Days in Nashville

Southwest cattle transport

Opt out at the airport, avoid radiation, but wait too long.
   Almost lose house keys, maybe wallet.
   Pat down

No wonder that dude shot TSA, the ultimate opt out.
   Pepsi ad: "Live for now." Worry about cancer from this
corrosive substance later.
   Rent an SUV.
   Check into the Omni.
   Get some BBQ.
   Downtown Broadway.
   Fifty shades of white.
   Every bum has a guitar.
   Every bar has a band.
   All country, all the time.
   Karaoke, Advil.
   RumChata, the titty milk of the gODs
   Merle Haggard

"Give me one reason to stay here, and I'll turn right back around."

Southern rock, CCR

An old man goes up to the karaoke mic and starts singing this:

I was gonna pay my car note until I got high
I wasn't gonna gamble on the boat but then I got high
now the tow truck is pulling away and I know why (why man?) yeah hey,
—because I got high
I was gonna make love to you but then I got high
I was gonna eat yo pussy too but then I got high
now I'm jacking off and I know why, yeah hey,
—'cause I got high
I messed up my entire life because I got high
I lost my kids and wife because I got high
now I'm sleeping on the sidewalk and I know why (why man?) yeah hey,
—'cause I got high

Beards, cowboy hats, and baseball caps.
    And that's just the ladies
    Flannel shirts, sequined belts, and high heels.
    And that's just the men
    Bleach-blonde bartenders. "Save a horse, ride a cowboy."

Has Kip Winger gone country?

Everyone traveling in packs. Packs of girls, packs of guys. Packs of blacks, packs of Arabs, well just one pack.

Pack of French men, one Asian girl

"Hey, Iron Man! Whatcha doin' in Nashville?"

Late-night diner.

Dry-rubbed BBQ sauce. Fat tater tots, fried green tomatoes.

Ooey-gooey baked yumminess

Middle Eastern girl in blackface getting faux-fucked by a man in a Confederate flag cape while another girl behind them makes it rain.

It's not a trailer park, it's a "trailer resort."

"The Bakersfield sound"

"In 1784 Nashborough became Nashville. The English 'borough' was replaced with the French 'ville,' most likely as a sign of appreciation for France's assistance during the American Revolution against Great Britain."

Andrew "Old Hickory" Jackson

Rapper Young Buck, Ca$hville, "Ten a key" just got outta prison!

"Ridin' in Ca$hville runnin' all stop lights. Homie is that real, I pray I keep livin'. My momma jus' had a dream of seein' me in prison."

Vanderbilt University

"Cry-in-your-beer songs"

Driving down Granny White Pike to Shackleford Road, Warfield Road to Free Beer Men's Consignment store

"Wouldn't it be grand?"

Honky-tonk
"I woke up in a new Bugatti."
Bluegrass, gospel, Cajun, western swing
Country rock, rockabilly
Bonnaroo
Chet Atkins, Patsy Cline.
CMA Awards
"And your high school sweetheart becomes your wife"
Meeting Facebook friends for the first time

Rippy's BBQ
"You're kind of indecisive, aren't you?"
Merchants Grill, Troubadours karaoke.
Ted's Montana Grill, poor bison!
Memphis is "rough around the edges."
"Redneck yacht club"
Piggly Wiggly
Apparently, people from west Florida have a southern accent.
I love bell-bottoms.
Kenny Chesney
Steel guitar, twelve-bar blues
Sounds like *Happy Days*
Fiddle, harmonica, accordion

Grand Ole Opry, sponsored by Humana
"Humana health plan is proud to be part of this Nashville tradition. Now for some birthdays."
"Now it's time for the Humana trivia challenge . . ."

No applause for the guy from New Orleans.

Six-string bass

Holding a guitar but not playing is a good look, like Bono

Banquet chicken advertisement while the band plays

"We call ourselves the White Girls."

This whole place is reminiscent of Frontierland at Disneyland, or maybe Country Bear Jamboree.

Use the capo!

The Smoky Mountains

Square dancing to fiddle music

Midair heel taps

"I put this album out myself since the recording companies in Nashville don't care about real country music."

—some cowboy

My stomach hurts.

Gaylord Entertainment Center

"You can't love me, baby, and love my brother too."

To my disappointment, no one is barefoot in overalls.

Forks and knives are our weapons.

Hermitage Cafe open all night till 1:00 p.m.

Biscuits and gravy, poor-boy sandwich

Homemade French coconut or pecan pie

Sweet tea

Chess pie and fried chicken for dessert?

Goo Goo with fresh roasted peanuts, caramel, marshmallow, and milk chocolate. A "nourishing lunch for a nickel." Can't find it. i'll order it on Amazon.

Twang Town
    Nashville Superspeedway
    1897 fairy floss spun into cotton candy

    "Never slow down, never grow old."

                  —Tom Petty

Podunk
    "You guys wanna go to a field party?"
    Kurdish Persian hookah palace
    Waiting two hours in the cold for the Bluebird Cafe
    (In heavy southern drawl) "I had two chairs in my truck, but I took 'em out before we left."
    Missed the ghetto tour of East Nashville and Antioch
    "It's a sad time when happy hour's over."

Funny and forlorn songs about jilted lovers

Ladies and gentlemen, Steve Goodie, country comedian:
    He opens with "The NASCAR Song":

Drive round and round and round and round and later you get paid

Go straight, take a left, take a left, go straight
Take a left, take a left, go straight
Drive round and round and round and round and
later you get lots of money

He closes with the "What's in My Hotdog" song:

No one seems to know, no one seems to know, no one
seems to want to know . . .
But I want to know, I got to know, oh I need to know
. . . what's in my hotdog
There's earlobes, eyelids, elbows, and fingertips
Dog nose, pig glands, frog bits, and chicken lips
Hog butts, peanuts, cow guts, brains . . .
Toe jam, turkey spam, varicose veins
What's in my hotdog, what's in my hotdog, what's in
my hotdog
No one wants to know
There's moose colon, horse bladder, anything that makes
a splatter
Half ton of puppy tongues, bucketful of camel lungs
Big hairy goat tails, dirty donkey toenails
Stuffed into a fabulous, edible, delectable, deep-fried,
something died . . . intestinal shell . . .
Intestinal shell . . .

End with Nashville City Cemetery.
Graves of slave masters and soldiers from the War of 1812.

We somehow escape Nashville and Southwest—cattle-flight it back to LA, where i plant my butt on my $4,000 Kohler Hatbox porcelain throne and proceed to explode diarrhea.

i think i'm going vegetarian after this.

The Doctors Have Sold Out

"Cardiologists Recommend Wider Use of Statin Drugs" is the title of an article in yesterday's *LA Times*. Nowhere in this article do they mention trying to be healthier by cutting down on meats, fast food, and smoking or increasing exercise—not even early screening for people with major family risk factors for heart disease.

Nope, just take more pills! How much money is to be made by adding thirty-five million people to the cholesterol pill market? But what about the side effects? "The writers of the new guidelines downplayed concerns about the medications' side effects. These include muscle aches and fatigue, a slight rise in blood sugar and, more rarely, hemorrhagic stroke and a toxic breakdown of muscle tissue called rhabdomyolysis."

Is it a coincidence that this is happening now, since "yearly spending on this class of drugs peaked at $21.3 billion in 2011, declining since then as more of those brand-name medications become available as generics"?

The defense of all this could be some top cardiologist saying, "Look, we're losing the battle. People are having strokes and heart attacks and don't give a shit about their diets and those other lifestyle modifications." That's fine. Then mention that. Put it in the article!

The *LA Times* basically posted a front-page ad for Big Pharma. Today, i am ashamed to be a doctor.

Think Outside the Line!

A dot is zero-dimensional. A line is one-dimensional. Two perpendicular lines, indicating length and width, are two-dimensional. Our vision, which includes depth, is three-dimensional. Contrary to claims of *The Twilight Zone* TV show, time is the fourth dimension. Most likely, undiscovered dimensions exist as well.

So how is it that the world of politics, which involves some of the most important aspects of our human experience, including war and power, is conceptualized as a simple one-dimensional line, with the left (liberals) on one end and the right (conservatives) on the other? All discussions of political ideas and leaders, whether they come from mindless TV or more notable authors, constantly refer to this simple one-dimensional line.

We need to think outside the line! Surely, all of us want to conserve some things and change other things. Can we not conceptualize a triangle? Now, you must be thinking i'm just some kind of geometry nut, but hold on. Refuse to accept our pseudo-two-party, one-dimensional system.

Why not ten parties, all dynamically changing with time, occupying four dimensions? If all this is too much for you, maybe we should just blow it all up and be left with *zero* dimensions.

Until next time, i'll see you in the Twilight Zone.

Dubre

We are in a cavernous spaceship, cozy with strange alien forms, hurling through black holes, viewing the entire experience through a five-story front windshield, night tripping. The sound of space brakes echoing through this chamber alerts the passengers on the main floor. They continue gyrating.

The captain is on deck, facing the crowd instead of the space window, pushing buttons and clicking, turning and twisting knobs. The engine ticks away at 130 beats per minute, too fat, much too fat.

A meteor shower flashes across the starboard windows. Some hairy aliens cheer. Piercing Martian LED-light eyeballs three feet apart rush to the bathroom.

Time is a melting faggot, a bundle of wood, that is.

i'm looking for a plank to take a nap on. Not now, but later, when i will be tired.

The first-class cabin is filled with interlopers now, loitering, soliciting, eavesdropping, going door to door with THIS INCREDIBLE OFFER!

i'm throwing ice cubes now, down at the Persians.

i meant plebeians. Pixelated crosses. It is becoming harder to write as i am being fondled.

Either the dress goes down or the curtain comes up.
Isn't it the other way around?
Either the dress goes up or the curtain comes down.
Checking pulses now, nonplussed.
Computers love water.

Fourth-Person Perspective

i am writing in the first person.
You are writing in the second person.
They are writing in the third person.
.nosrep htruof eht ni gnitirW

Playa del Carmen

"This will do."

      —at Hotel Las Palapas

"It's raining; i should have stayed home."

      —at Aeropuerto Internacional de Cancún

My hotel bungalow comes with its own nativity scene. i knew Jesus (Hay-Zeus) was Mexican.

"Tourist trap."

      —at Tulum, Península de Yucatán

"Vendors selling water on the dance floor; America, take note."

      —at Blue Parrot

i feel sorry for the old American couple at the front desk complaining about the interminable BOOM BOOM BOOM BOOM of bass coming from the BPM Festival next door and the incessant downpour of tropical rain, a rain that, forty years ago, would have been an excuse to skip their planned tourist excursions and, instead, roll around in their beach bungalow, a rain that now holds up these hexagenerians as prisoners in this fogged-up, migraine-inducing "resort."

Perhaps i would have enjoyed my sunset swim in the warm Caribbean waters of the Mexican Riviera if i could not smell the putrid putrefaction of digested animal carcasses released by thousands of tourists' large intestines overgrown with foreign bacteria, the smell of partially absorbed white-corn gruel, fish heads, a blizzard of gizzards, frat-boy Jose Cuervo and Jägermeister vomit, semen, and vaginal fluid oozing from used condoms flushed into the sewage complex, and the taste of all the above, sloshed around in turbulent seas like it was Poseidon's blender, then introduced into any of my orifices, such as my ears, nostrils, and occasionally opened mouth as i attempted to take a breath while swimming.

Perhaps . . .

One can never bring enough business cards into third-world countries.

Late-night grub session at Don Sirloin Tacos.

"The reason many palm tree trunks are painted white is to prevent insects from climbing the trees. The whitewash has a lime base added to it. It is also used as a warning sign to drivers that there is a tree there."

i was about to ask a group of girls if i could join in on their beach volleyball until i realized they were playing with their feet.

What is the difference between *cochinita* and *puerco*?

Cave dining at Alux Caverna Restaurant Lounge.

Sayonara, Mexico! Oh, wait—that's Japanese. No wonder i was having such language problems.

Picture Baby Jason Rollin'

Picture me rollin' in my dad's Lexus SUV

I got love no matter who you be since there's so much need

My folks got me under surveillance, that's what my Uncle B be tellin'

Know there's milk bein' sold, but I ain't the one sellin'!

Don't want to be another number

I got a smurfin' gang of cousins to keep from goin' under

The rival babies wanna see me wet my bed—but don't worry, I got lead for their heads

I'm talking about a No. 2 pencil, Mom! Writing poems by my bed,

Now I'm released without a car seat, how will I live? Will Daddy forgive me

For all the poop a baby did, are you gonna clean it?

One life to live, it's so hard to be negative

When my whole fam be partying at my crib.

Song Titles of Some Death Metal Band

"The Pulsating Feast"
"Domination through Mutilation"
"Escort Service of the Dead"
"Obscene Body Slayings"
"Fecal Freak"
"Humiliated in Your Own Blood"
"Just Another Stillborn"
"Parade of the Decapitated Midgets"
"Ruptured Remains in a Doggie Bag"
"Copious Head Carnage"
"Carnivorous Erection"
"Relentless Pursuit of Rotting Flesh"
"Swallow the Human Filth"
"Dismantle the Afterbirth"
"Choked in Shit"
"Funeral Genocide"
"Rancid Head of Splatter"
"Rage against Humanity"
"To Boil a Corpse"

"Bloody Pile of Human Waste"
"Drenched in Cattle Blood"
"Carbonated Death"
"Skull of Shit and Sludge"
"Desperate Need for Violation"
"Thirty-Seven Stab Wounds"
"Vomified (Regurgitated to the Core)"
"Headless She Died"
"Breath Like Rotten Meat"
"I Wanna Kill"
"Claw-Hammer Castration"
"Festering Embryonic Vomit"
"Smeared with Blood-Mixed Semen"
"You're about to Fuckin' Die"
"Stinking Genital Warts"
"Pyronecrobestiality"
"Self-Disembowelment"
"Savage Gore Whore"
"The Combustion and Consumption of Pyorrheic Waste"

To Pee or Not to Pee

To pee, or not to pee: that is the question:
Whether 'tis nobler in the mind to suffer
The gimps and the limps of outrageous fellatio,
Or to take antibiotic lotion against a sea of titties, nay,
"ta-tas"
And by opposing sharts end to end? To die: to sleep;
Fap no more; and by a sleep to say we end
The hard-on and the thousand natural cocks
That tumescent flesh is hairy too, 'tis masturbation
Devoutly to be wish'd. To die a bit, to orgasm;
To sleep: perchance to wet dream: ay, there's the part
where i rub one out;
For in that sleep of death what dreams may cum on ye
When we have fluffed off this turtle-head,
Must give us anal prolapse: there's the respect
That makes prostitution of so long a cock-wife;
For who would bear the leather whips and paddles of
time,
The masochist's wrong, the proud man's sodomy,
The venereal warts of despised love, the vaginal walls'
delay,

The insolence of orifices and the sperm
That patient's burning of the unholy shakes,
When he himself might his coitus make
With a bare blumpkin? Who would fart on her,
To grunt and sweat under a weary wife,
But that the dread of something after climax,
The undiscover'd country from whose pubes
No traveler returns, puzzles the will
And makes us rather bear those genitourinary ills we have
Than fly to others that we know not of? Whores?
Thus consummation does make cowards of us all;
And thus the native, purple veiny hue of erection
Is sicklied o'er with the pale cast of her white ass,
And enterprises of burning piss this moment
With this regard their urine currents turn awry,
And lose the name of action.
—Soft you now!
The fair Council! Nymph, in thy ovaries
Be all my sins remember'd.

Playa del Carmen, Part 2

"Excuse me, garçon, i would like to buy those girls a round of drinks."

"Ahh, very good sir. Which girls?"

"Those three girls, there. The only ones sitting by themselves."

"OK, sir. What would you like? Perhaps piña colada?"

"Whatever they are drinking."

"OK, very good, sir."

"Excuse me, garçon. What happened? You didn't order the girls any drinks. Oh, now look—they've ordered themselves margaritas. Go tell them i will pay for those drinks."

"Very good, sir. You would like to buy them a round of drinks?"

"What? Yes, those drinks there. Go tell them those drinks are on me."

"Perhaps some piña coladas?"

"What? No. It's too late for that. They already have margaritas. No one wants piña coladas after margaritas. Just go tell them that i am paying for those margaritas that they already have in front of them. Hurry up now, the window of opportunity is closing."

"Very good, sir."

(Waiter talks to ladies. Ladies look over. i hold up my drink in a toast motion. Ten minutes later, ladies finish their drinks and walk past me on the way out.)

Ladies: You are an asshole. The waiter was demanding that we buy you a piña colada.

Occupy Wolf of Wall Street

Who the fuck recommended this movie?

Was it you?

i distinctly remember someone saying that this movie was not a glorification of Jordan Belfort, the stock market trickster who swindled hardworking Americans for millions of dollars with *Boiler Room*–type, "pump-and-dump," sham investments. i specifically avoided purchasing this DVD (please don't fucking tell me you saw it in the theater) so as not to contribute to this sneaky fucker making any more money. After all, the only real voice we have in this inverse totalitarian society is with our pocketbooks.

So when a friend of mine who already foolishly purchased the DVD suggested we watch it, i tentatively agreed. Well, hey, guess what? This movie *was* a complete glorification of Belfort, after all. He was the hero. The FBI agents were the villains (OK, i like that idea). i kept waiting for the moral lesson to come, but it never did. What? You mean that one-minute scene near the end where he serves twenty-two months at a federal tennis camp? Some lesson.

"But Leonardo DiCaprio is such a good actor," you say. What the fuck does that exactly mean? He is realistic? Regular people walking on the street are realistic. They are *real* people doing *real* things. DiCaprio is *acting*. He's doing a little song and dance like a clown for $20 million, thanks to your contribution. He is entertaining us. *Are you not entertained?*

So is that good enough? This "good" actor, along with Scorsese, a "good" director with a hard-on for real-life criminals, totally glamorize Belfort's life, and we just sit there like the little fucking automaton couch potatoes that we are and take it (up the ass, why not?).

"Calm down," you say. "It's just entertainment. I'm a good person," you say. "After a hard day at work, I like to just kick back and watch a movie," you say. "No big deal, I can afford fifteen dollars."

No big deal? You can afford it? Remember that little $700-billion-plus bailout of the banking industry by the US government with taxpayer money back in 2008? Remember how many people defaulted on their mortgages and lost their homes, only to find out later that the big banks had a complicit role in shady and illegal subprime mortgage schemes, CDOs, and a bunch of other stuff? The big banks have since then paid billions in fines, but no one, NOT ONE FUCKING PERSON, went to jail. It turned out that WAS a big deal, and we as a nation could *not* afford it.

So what does any of this have to do with watching Jordan Belfort's movie about his life? It has to do with exactly the same thing. Financially supporting economic terrorists, whether it's a fifteen-dollar DVD or an account at Bank Robbers of America, pushes us as a nation (nay, as a planet) one step closer to the precipice (insert fiscal cliff joke here).

So what can you do? Stop spending your fucking money on this shit! i don't care how charming DiCaprio is or how Fellini-esque Scorsese's cinematography is (which it's not). This is *Goodfellas* meets Gordon Gekko's *Wall Street*. Don't spend your money on these economic hitmen.

Look, i like a good drug orgy as much as the next guy. But personally, i would rather be in my own *real* one than watch a ridiculously exaggerated one in a pompous movie. But what the fuck do i know, anyway? i'm not a *New York Times* reporter. i'm not Siskel or Ebert (aren't they both dead?). The only negative review of this movie i found was a complaint about the number of times the word *fuck* was used. i've been fucking emulating that here. Do you fucking like it? Fucker. So who am i? i am just like you, a nobody. And everybody. We are the masses, and with the era of the internet, we finally have a voice.

Since Occupy Wall Street and the Move Your Money Project, over $5 billion has been moved out of the big banks. Imagine what we could do to Hollywood with that same type of galvanization. Imagine if we boycotted the Holly-wood bullshit. OK, my polemic is done.

Now go watch *Zeitgeist* or something.

Li'l Zé, the Brazilian Pickpocket

Oi! Tudo bem? Por favor, excuse my Inglês. Meu nome is Li'l Zé, and I am a twelf-year-old Carioca. That means a person from Rio de Janeiro. I live in a slum, *favela*, and right now, *agora*; I am walking along the *famosa* Copacabana beach. I looking for *turista* to steal money. This is best time of night. It is about *dois*, 2:00 a.m., and the gringos are drunk, coming out of the bars. You can't see my two friends who are hiding over there in the shadows by the beach. The black one is Acerola, and the brown one is Laranjinha. Both of them are twelf like me. I know them my whole life. We are good team.

Bom! There is one! I see a man, maybe Spanish, walking outside Club Help. That is a whorehouse. He has a goatee. He looks like that Iron Man movie star. Or maybe his retarded *irmão*. Fuck him. He is wearing a T-shirt and baggy American short pants. Big pockets. Those are the easiest to steal out of. He is wearing funny big black *Japonês* boots. He can't chase us with those shoes. *Gato?* Is that a cat walking next to him? Yes! And he's talking to it!

"Looks like it's just you and me again, Orwell," he says.

Como louco! He's talking to a gato! I give a short bird whistle to let Acerola and Laranjinha know this is the one. He's drunk, walking in the alley, and talking to his gato.

Bom! At the same time Acerola sneaks up behind him and kneels sideways behind his legs, Laranjinha walks up to him and says, "Meester, Meester. Por favor. Give me money. *Dinheiro.*"

The gringo says, "Oh shit, i'm getting jacked!" He backs up and trips over Acerola, who is behind him. He falls on ground. I run up. I stick my hand in his big pocket. Bam! Moolah! I run away with the money. Acerola and Laranjinha run to different streets. I look back at the man, and I see his eyes. He is not scared or angry. He looks sad. I understand something in his eyes.

Now he is chasing me! I run faster. I don't know how he runs with those crazy Japonês boots. I look back again. His gato is running with him. But then the cat gets stuck in his feet, and they both fall down. *Até lago.* See you later, sucker! I meet Acerola and Laranjinha at our spot next to the bus stop. We count our treasure: 666 reals. That is about $300 US. We split it three ways. There is also a letter. Acerola says I should read it because my Inglês is best. On the bus back to Rocinha Favela, I read the letter out loud. This is what is says:

Congratulations! You have successfully pickpocketed the world-famous word DJ Ass Maggots. i consider this an honor and place you as the best of the best. No hard feelings. The politics of poverty and national income disparity are complicated, but i imagine your country has a similar history to other "third-world" countries—a history that is rooted in the aftermath of slavery and likely is more recently a financial victim of the United States' high-interest loan scams, disguised as financial aid from the World Bank and the International Monetary Fund, which place a few powerful families in pecuniary heaven while impoverishing the middle class. Or maybe your country is just a victim of blatant corruption by its own power elite. i hope you at least are able to enjoy the money you jacked from me before you, yourself, become a victim of a violent crime, which is also endemic in conditions of squalor.

i have clipped a red capsule to the bottom of this page. It is 2C-B, a psychedelic "medicine" that will connect your cerebral cortex to the universe and help you see how the world really works. You can find me at www.DJAssMaggots.com. *Tchau!*

I no understand most of what I read, and Acerola and Larajinha fall asleep. Later, I walk up the hill in Rocinho favela to my family's home. It is two small rooms with pieces of metal from a factory as the walls and roof. I give my grandmother, *minha avó*, one hundred reals so she can buy her *medicinas*. She almost die last time her medicinas empty. I give mi mother, *minha mãe*, one hundred reals so she can pay the rent, so the drug lords don't kick us out again. They don't ask me where I got the money. My younger brother, my two sisters, and my auntie live here too. I save twenty reals for myself. I will buy ice cream for me and my *companheiros* tomorrow.

I think about that funny gringo. I should invite him to the favela. My uncle needs a kidney. Just kidding. "Or not," as the Americans say. I open the letter again. I swallow the red pill.

Twice Your Age

Remember when i was twice your age, when you were seventeen and i was thirty-four, when your dad was trying to get me arrested for statutory rape?

Remember when you were twenty-seven and i was forty-four, when we got married and everyone thought you were a gold digger?

Remember when you were thirty-seven and i was fifty-four, when the doctor said you were too old to have a baby? They were wrong two more times after that.

Remember when you were forty-seven and i was sixty-four, when you took over your company and i retired from mine?

Remember when you were fifty-seven and I was seventy-four, when our college-age daughter surprised us by making us grandparents?

Remember when you were sixty-seven and i was eighty-four, when i was on my deathbed and i gave you my blessings to date my good friend Arthur, who always had the hots for you and was a spry seventy-five?

Remember when I was twice your age? No? I don't, and nobody else does either.

T,S,A,

So i'm standing in the opt-out-of-radiation corner with plenty of time before my flight, watching all the stressed-out people of every ethnicity wrestle each other for plastic bins to put their shoes, backpacks, unobstructed laptops, and other carry-on items into, when the overworked TSA lady handling the boarding passes and IDs yells in the general direction of the TSA guys in front of the X-ray machines.

"We need to open up another line. It's too crazy over here."

"Slow down!" yells back the TSA guy next to me, the guy who's shortly going to be running the back of his blue-gloved hands suspiciously close to my scrotum.

"Who said that?" responds the wretched TSA lady with an animated movement of her head. She glares at me with exophthalmos bulging eyes.

"I said it!" says the same classy TSA gentleman next to me.

"Oh no you didn't," she responds, menacingly waving her overly manicured hands with fake nails, like a *Jerry Springer* guest right before an attack.

Everyone goes quiet for a beat.

"What are you laughing at?" my TSA groper asks.

"You guys are awesome." i laugh. "'Merica!"

The Happiest Day

It was a cold winter day one morning in a small town in western Iran near the borders of Iraq and Turkey. This town was known mainly for the strange accent of its people, which distinguished them every time they spoke Farsi. It was a town with no more than a few thousand people, a town where everyone knew everyone else, a town without secrets, and an honest town where one could pay for milk when one had money to buy milk.

The occupants of this town had made an effort to keep their old traditions of simple life despite the city's push to join the big metropolitan world. Most people were teachers and employees of some government firm or bank nine months out of the year, but during the three months of summer, they were all farmers. Farmers who got up before dawn to milk the cows and collect the eggs; farmers who gathered in their little farmhouses after sunset with their sons and daughters and had dinner. For these summer farmers, every meal was a feast, a feast without a reason for a feast. In their farms and gardens surrounding the town, there was no television or VCR; in fact, not all had electricity. What every house had, however, were people with open doors and open arms, an invitation for others to come without an invitation. People gathered at night and talked, talked of weather, talked of politics, talked of the world news and city gossip.

Alex was born in this small town, but soon after his birth, his parents took him to Tehran, hoping that life in the big city would bring him a better future. The big city, though, had little chance to offer him anything. Soon after they moved, Tehran became the target of relentless destruction by the neighboring country, Iraq. Twelve years after his birth, the heavy city bombings forced Alex and his mother to return to the small town, which had remained untouched by the enemy planes and their bombs, perhaps because of its close proximity to Turkey.

So it was indeed a cold winter day one morning in a city west of Iran. Alex was a new student in an all-boys middle school, as gender segregation was mandatory in all schools, including universities. While on the third floor in a chemistry laboratory that morning, he heard the siren's scream. Alex was well familiar with this sound, and he knew well that he needed to stay away from windows and hide underneath a table with his face down; so he did. Others, however, stood still in disbelief of enemy planes flying over their skies. Their town had no military or political significance. But their disbelief was soon replaced by terror as the first storm of bombs shocked the city. Windows shattered and buildings shook. Alex followed the wave of screaming children that headed for the stairs and onto the streets.

The scene was horrible, worse than any nightmare. This was really happening. Buildings he had seen standing, old yet strong, now burned in fire, and inside these buildings, people lay silent and dead, and those who had little life left in them screamed as their bodies flamed to ashes. The dead were everywhere, in every corner of every street, the young and the old, with stories never to be told. The usual bright-blue sky of the town was now covered with the black cloud of smoke and fire. Today, on this cold winter day, the fire of burning buildings lit the city, and the sun hid behind the cloud of smoke and flames, as if ashamed by the nature of humanity.

Chaos filled the streets. People were running, all running in tears, all running without a destination, running with fear, running with the hope that the house burning on their street was their neighbor's and not theirs, hoping that the dead child lying in the corner was their friend's son and not theirs. That cold winter day in this small city west of Iran, many sons and daughters died, many sons and daughters became orphans, and many families became homeless.

Sirens were still sounding, but now they cried rather than screamed. Alex entered the street and looked around. He felt lost and confused. He needed a reminder of yesterday's life to wake him from his nightmare. He looked at people, the people he knew, the same people who gave him milk and bread every day, the same people who taught him mathematics and history every day, the same people who sat next to him every day and walked home with him every day. But he recognized none of those people. All the familiar faces now looked strange.

His heart raced nearly out of his chest, beating faster than it ever had. He found a surge of energy, and soon he joined the crowd of runners. He started running. He ran fast, and the faster he ran, the less real his nightmare became. The faster he ran, the more familiar his friends became; the faster he ran, the less dead were the children in the corners. And so he ran, running nowhere but away from his confused mind. He ran through the burning houses, he ran past burning cars, and he ran over burning mothers holding their burning children. He ran until he could no longer run, and then he ran some more.

In the midst of the rust-colored sky and smoke-filled air, he recognized the figure of a stranger. He could not make out a clear picture through the cloud of smoke, but in that chaos, her movements looked familiar. She was running aimlessly toward him. He looked down at her feet and saw the familiarity, the one reminder of yesterday's life, which would bring him back to reality. She was wearing his tennis shoe on one foot and her red sandal on the other foot. Mother. She was breathing fast and irregularly, and her hands were shaking. And yet with all her disarray, she calmed Alex down. Once more he found safety in his mother's arms; once more her one touch made all of his nightmares disappear, even if it was only for a moment.

In that one moment, he found happiness. He found happiness as his friends died. He found happiness as his friends became orphans. He found happiness in a world now filled with sadness. But that day his happiness was much stronger than any bomb the human race could ever make. That day his happiness could give life to a forest in a desert. That cold winter day, in that small town in western Iran, his happiness made him smile. He and his mother were alive, and that fact alone made this his happiest day.

—by Alireza Fathi, MD

Illuminous Pyramid

i'm down. Put the green and the white stuff down.
i'm on a Playa bike with my tits out.
Girrrrl, come hang with the real Gs.
Behind Center Camp, Rod's Road orgy.
Or find me on the Esplanade
Riding dark, behind the cop cars,
Snorting K on the monkey bars,
Dosin' Abel with G in his drink jar.
Bruh, if you can't handle Goner with his cock out
Ya might need to get the fuck out.

—Burning Man, 2016

Dear Immigrant

Please turn around and go back to where you came from. America has no more room for you. We have our own poor people to deal with, not that we have ever cared about them until just right now.

What's that? You're running here because we have turned your country into a full-scale drug-war zone because of our insistence on keeping marijuana, cocaine, methamphetamine, and other drugs illegal while simultaneously providing the necessary black-market demand in the form of millions of American users? And you say all the guns used in the bloodshed of your own people come from America? Well, I'll have to check the record and get back to you. And besides, I don't do drugs, so it's not my problem (except for Ritalin, Adderall, Lidocaine, Novocain, and legalized hemp).

Is immigration a new issue, you ask? Yes, it is, because they're talking about it on TV. What about the Italians, Irish, Jews, and Greeks, you ask? Well, that's old news, and they're already here. Besides, they're of European descent, just like most Americans. And I'm not even talking about the blacks. Slavery was a long time ago and has absolutely nothing to do with their sorry situation. They should stop asking for handouts and go get a job. Am I hiring? Umm . . . I'll have someone get back to you on that.

What's that? America has destabilized your country, and you have no choice but to move your family away from conflict? For the record, America has *never* destabilized a country. We bring democracy! (Except for Korea 1950–1953, Iran 1953, Guatemala 1954, Indonesia 1958, Cuba 1959, Dominican Republic 1961, Congo 1965, Iraq 1963, South Vietnam 1963 and the Vietnam War 1955–1975, Brazil 1964, Ghana 1966, Chile 1973, Argentina 1976, Turkey 1980, Poland 1981, Afghanistan 1980s, Nicaragua 1980s, Cambodia 1980s, Angola 1980s, Iraq again in the 1990s, Afghanistan 2001, Venezuela 2002, Iraq again 2003, Haiti 2004, Gaza Strip 2006, Somalia 2006, Libya 2011, Syria 2012, and Yemen 2015.)

Whew! I guess all these people come here because we're the best. No, I've never been to any of those places. Actually, I don't even have a passport. I haven't even left my home state, except for Vegas, of course. Look, I'm not a racist. I have a black friend *and* a Mexican one.

Xenophobe? Jingoist? I'm sorry, I don't speak French.

What's that? Why am I not forming a border patrol against Saudis, who were linked to 9/11? Well, they fly in by plane, and it's kind of pointless to build a wall at an airport. Besides, that's oil money. We *need* that.

It's so much easier to just build a wall against Mexico. Walls are good, right? Look at the Berlin wall. Look at the

Israel/Palestinian wall. Anyway, southern states are eager to help, and you know they're usually on the *right* side of history.

Sincerely,

Concerned American

Dear Concerned American

I am writing back to you on this phone that an old person from your country no longer needs. They moved to my country to retire, buying up some of the best land on the beach where my parents used to take me when I was three years old. Now that I am not so little, we cannot go to that beach anymore because they threaten to shoot us. Also, my parents are in your country, and that is the problem.

My mother told me she would call for my sister and me when she gets enough money for us. She came to your country because that is where she said the jobs are now. She left five years ago.

Now that I am thirteen, I have to feed my sister and my brother. But the home we stay in, with the metal roof, it has no door, and the men say we have to pay them or they will do bad things to my sister, like they did to my aunt and my cousin.

I ask them if I can help them to get money, and they laugh because they say all the money comes from your country and goes to the *traficantes*, unless I want to kill someone to show them.

I don't want to kill someone. And I don't want them to hurt my sister or my brother or me.

So I have to come there and find my mother. I know she is there.

I don't know why she has not called for us yet. Maybe because the phones are so bad here.

We only have to take the train through Mexico. I have saved some food, and my friend tells me he is leaving tomorrow. He is almost fifteen, and he knows a lot, so I will take my brother and sister, and we will ride the trains with him.

I have made a knife from some cans, so we will be protected. I pray to God to watch us on the journey. We should be able to avoid the coyotes. I know God will help us because my daddy is up there with him, and he will watch us too. I think you get your head back when you go to heaven.

Anyway, American, I hope things are not as bad as you say there. Is your sister being raped and your brothers' heads cut off too? Because if that is happening, maybe we should go somewhere else.

Besides, Americans love children, like in Disneyland. Maybe my mother will take us there when we see her. I always love Mickey Mouse.

I have to run.

Ahi nos vemos!

(sent from some dead American's iPhone)

—LPR

Dear Concerned American and Concerned Immigrant

What the fuck does any of this nonsense have to do with things that really matter: the World Cup? How can anyone care about such minutiae when Lionel Messi's reputation is in jeopardy due to his lackluster performance in the final? Will Cristiano Ronaldo continue his struggles in the World Cup while putting up tremendous numbers for Real Madrid? Will Brazil rebound from its horrendous World Cup performance on its own soil? How will the rules committee deal with concussion issues as well as continued diving in the penalty box?

Please stop whining about world hunger, war, climate pollution, financial and social inequality, global banking, and all your other petty issues. Stick only to the *futbol* questions I presented, and leave the rest of the garbage out.
Sincerely,
Unconcerned former immigrant and now an American citizen

—Night Writer, Esq.

Music Video Shoot

Friday night. Downtown LA. An empty park.

11:30 p.m.: i show up at designated address in Lamborghini. i find a locked gate and no one around.

11:35 p.m.: First car of *vatos* pulls up to me. They are wasted. Bunch of car talk.

11:45 p.m.: Second car of vatos. Face tattoos. i tell them i'm producing a music video. Give them my IG info.

11:55 p.m.: Cops pull up. Ask what i'm doing. i say i'm just cruising around. They nod to the street sign right next to me that says No Cruising Allowed. i tell them i'm not cruising. They ask how fast the car goes.

Midnight: The guys for the video find me. i leave my car next to a temporary tow-away sign, but we hide the sign behind a tree.

12:30 a.m.: i hike a random trail up a hill in the dark. i join the video already in progress.

2:00 a.m.: We all come back down to the Lamborghini, which is still there.

2:30 a.m.: i teach Braxton how to drive a paddle-shifter-only Lamborghini, which is hard to start, has major blind spots, has a poor turning radius, is difficult to e-brake, and is tricky to reverse.

2:35 a.m.: Another group of vatos in a muscle car pulls up to us while we're practicing parking. They offer us huge balloons that they're inhaling. We decline.

2:45 a.m.: Cops pull up. i come up with a ridiculous backstory. They ask how fast the car goes.

3:00 a.m.: After convincing the crew and actors not to run away, Braxton drives the Lamborghini for the video.

4:00 a.m.: We all say goodbye at a gas station, but then we come across a cat that has just been hit by a car. Another cat won't leave the side of the dying cat. We block other cars from hitting the cats. We place the newly dead cat next to a tree and offer it back to Mother Earth.

4:20 a.m.: Cops pull me over in the Lamborghini. i tell them i'm lost, and they direct me to the nearest on-ramp. They ask how fast the car goes.

5:00 a.m.: i go to sleep.

The LAX Airport Dog

As i was going through LAX customs and baggage claim, a little security dog started barking at me and jumped at my backpack. The customs agent lady/dog handler asked me if i had an apple in there. i did, actually!

i got sent to the special line. To save them search time, i took out my apple and started eating it. When i got to the front and handed the lady my slip, she laughed and said, "And you're eating the apple! We'll have to take that away." Then they x-rayed my baggage, and i was free to go.

On the way out, i saw other people really getting the third degree, like squeezing out toothpaste tubes and body checks.

i would like to thank the dog for barking "apple" instead of "rectal."

Is There a Doctor on the Plane?

Just like Morocco, i was disturbed from my business-class slumber on the way back from Greece by a call for assistance for a passenger with chest pain.

This time it was a fifty-four-year-old female from Jordan with cardiac risk factors. But it appeared the two glasses of red wine she had were the problem. Her blood pressure would drop when she tried to stand. We would have run some IV fluids, but we didn't have a nurse with us this time.

We didn't need to land early, and the patient was OK. *Opa!*

I, Too, Am Vegan

I am vegan
    On the inside,
    Weakened by a heart
    Made only of flesh,
    Further strained,
    Disemboweled
    By its bowels full
    Of pig, and bleating lamb
    Circumpressed down to nuggets like coal,
    Dense with energy, but so foul,
    So full of fowl
    I can hear them now, see them staring in uncomprehend-
    ing horror
    But I shut the door behind the eye-watering
    Visions of flayed feathers and them gaping and blind,
    Into the mouthwatering flavors, the smells, the sights,
    To savor the savoir-faire of
    Modern gastronomy
    —I'm addicted, you see
    As surely as coke, crack, Vic/Oxy, ecstasy can make you
want a pill or three—

To the fleshly delights earthy: the spices, the colors, the veggies surrounding, compounding, sometimes confounding the fatty, sinewy, marbled musclery, the fabulously melting and chewy burst of pleasure centrally with every stroke counterclockwise mandibularly.

—juices oh so juiciest juicy—and the creamy, dreamy

— -/- —.'/' — ,/, — -/- —

And that's no excuse, of course, for this cruel, vicious, unnecessary intercourse of mouth to myotome—

Yet ask an addict to anything you think that's addictive and come back to me—that's how I feel, you see

So I ask you, dear vegan,

Hear my confession and my plea

Perhaps you were once a lot like me

Or just a kebab or clam chowder away,

once again:

To. Be . . .

Unclean,

Uncaring

Unwholesome (But "manly")

But not

Unwilling!

Perhaps some genes lean more one way than another

And perhaps like many other -alities, it metabolizes as it pleases

And perhaps some were just born with a propensity toward tissue or weed

So many different types of seed and seeding and seedlings

Must be some other way to slake this need

So if you must hurt me, harm me—do what you see think needs be

But then don't just leave me, help me, or at least show me, the way toward a life

(mostly) murder-free.

Many thanks to thee

Your friend, if you'll have me

—Written by my good friend, Jerry Curls,

a.k.a. LPR, August 31, 2018

The Council: Leviticus

Son, see this egg? This is your brain. Now see me put this egg up my ass? That's your brain in the Council. Any questions?

If one word sums me up, it's *nothing*.

Asian Deep-Dish Orgy, MILF Revolution, Lesbo Pool Party, Erotic Threesomes, Home-Made Sex Tapes 2, Best Anal of 2013, The Lust Resort, Fresh Picked, MILFs Get It Their Way, Don't Tell My Husband 2, Dirty Rotten Mothers, My Husband Brought Home His Mistress 2 . . .

Soft LED lights.

No one writes a seven-hundred-page treatise because they were happy.

When visiting Seattle, don't make fun of a guy's man-bag until you know the contents. Washington State's concealed carry laws are very loose.

YODO: you only die once.

"Use of force was authorized" is such a sweet, passive, Orwellian phrase to use instead of "I decided to kill someone with my gun."

No pain, no pain.

Taro and boba.

> "The United States is a very young nation, and is even newer at being a dominant global power. Like a young and powerful adolescent, it tends to become disproportionately emotional about events that are barely remembered a few years later. Lebanon, Panama, Kuwait, Somalia, Haiti, Bosnia, and Kosovo all seemed at the time to be extraordinarily important and even decisive.
>
> "The reality is that few people remember them— and when they do, they cannot clearly define what drew the United States into the conflict in the first place. The emotionalism of the moment exhausts itself rapidly.
>
> "The crucial flip side to this phenomenon is that the Lebanese, Panamanians, Kuwaitis, Somalis, Haitians, Bosnians, and Kosovars all remember their tangles with American power for a long time. What was a passing event for the United States becomes a defining moment in the other countries' histories.
>
> "Here we discover the first and crucial asymmetry of the twenty-first century. The United States has

global interests and involves itself in a large number of global skirmishes. No one involvement is crucial. For the countries that are the object of American interest, however, any intervention is a transformative event. Frequently the object nation is helpless in the face of the American actions, and that sense of helplessness breeds rage even under the best of circumstances. The rage grows all the more when the object of the rage, the United States, is generally both invulnerable and indifferent. The twenty-first century will see both American indifference to the consequences of its actions and the world's resistance and anger toward America."

—George Friedman, *The Next 100 Years: A Forecast for the 21st Century* (2009)

"Iranians don't have bad hair days; they have less-than-fabulous hair days."

Misconceptions regarding Frankenstein's monster: Mary Shelley's version was created in an apartment, not a castle or dungeon. "It's alive!" never happened. The monster spoke elegantly, just like his creator and everyone else in the book— no grunting or growling.

What you call advertising, i call graffiti. What you call graffiti, i call art.

"Thank God for the rain, which has helped wash away the garbage and trash off the sidewalks . . . All the animals come out at night—whores, skunk pussies, buggers, queens, fairies, dopers, junkies, sick, venal. Someday a real rain will come and wash all this scum off the streets. I go all over. I take people to the Bronx, Brooklyn, I take 'em to Harlem. I don't care. Don't make no difference to me. It does to some. Some won't even take spooks. Don't make no difference to me.

"Each night when I return the cab to the garage, I have to clean the cum off the back seat. Some nights, I clean off the blood."

— *Taxi Driver* (1976)

"I completely fell in love on the dance floor at Burning Man. I was rocking out in the DJ booth with my favorite DJ. Like, dancing and going crazy. And then the next thing I know, I'm on the dance floor with this man who has the most stunning green eyes. And we're dancing, and I swear to you it was love at first dance. And it was brilliant, and it was sexy, and it was just, like, so connected . . . but it could have just been the molly."

—LushBunny

i think i'm going to become one of those writers you don't hear about in school. (Note lowercase "i" signifying humility.)

"Every country gets the circus it deserves: Spain gets bullfights. Italy gets the Catholic Church. America gets Hollywood."

—Erica Jong, *How to Save Your Own Life*

Sports? Athletes? The entire market of sports in our modern world has reached ridiculous levels. It is truly sad that there is even so much money being funneled from hardworking people into this entertainment industry. Advertising and TV as a whole continue to dupe the masses. We are all part of the problem. Kobe Bryant walks into a restaurant, and everyone goes nuts. No one ever went nuts for my high school calculus teacher. And he was pretty good. Kobe is a grown man who tosses inflated animal skins through iron rings for a living. How absurd is that?

"In 1492 native Americans found Columbus lost at sea."

"All I want is a living. It's all any honest man wants."
—slave trader, 1852

GREETINGS, VAPID COUNCIL MEMBERS AND UNHOLY MOTHERFUCKERS. Release the three-eyed AIDS-infested prairie mice and prepare for another week on this mud-ball guest planet called Earth. i love you all! Judy, make me another fuckin' drink.

You can't have orgies, then claim to be goth. Goth comes from a fundamental lack of companionship, a loathsomeness.

"Those who don't build must burn."
—Ray Bradbury, *Fahrenheit 451*

Congress shall make no law respecting an establishment of religion other than Christianity, or prohibiting the questionably free exercise thereof; or abridging the freedumb of speech of the press, as they will censor themselves; or the right of the people peaceably to assemble until 10:00 p.m. with a permit, and to petition the government wastebasket for redress of grievances.

Thou doth dicketh around too much.

"The great question that has never been answered, and which I have not yet been able to answer, despite my thirty years of research into the feminine soul, is What does a woman want?"

—Sigmund Freud

Um, probably a guy who doesn't want to bang his mom.

"I am a gay Catholic Marxist artist."

—Pasolini

"Without government you cannot exist, as they're the ones that protect you from imaginary threats, extend their hands in your best interest around the world and topple governments in the name of your way of life . . . oh and they make stamps, flags, monuments and shit."

—Kray Kray

Why are you getting all excited because the lotto is $200 million? Does $20 million not do it for you? Are you planning on buying the Lakers? What about $1 million? Is that just change under your couch?

Give me a fucking break. The only reason you care about $200 million is because everyone is hyping it up. Mob mentality.

i'll give you a little hint. The best you will ever do is win a couple hundred bucks. And that's after you've spent a couple hundred bucks on lotto tickets. You're going nowhere.

i'll see you at the Black Friday sale beating up old ladies for cheap microwaves.

i am inexorably incorrigible.

An **iconoclast** is someone who engages in iconoclasm— destruction of religious symbols or, by extension, established dogma or conventions.

> "I slept with faith and found a corpse in my arms on awakening; I drank and danced all night with doubt and found her a virgin in the morning."
> —Aleister Crowley

1. All societies have some "oppressed people" who are less fortunate than others.
2. I cannot change the system, but I'll just try to do my best within the system.

These two points illustrate how one might not support people who lost their homes from the Wall Street mortgage disaster, or Chinese workers rights, or the abolition of African slavery in the last millennium, or countless other examples of varying degrees of social depravity.

i don't want a "memory-foam" pillow. i want a "let-me-forget-everything" pillow.

You think your silly Halloween decor outside your house is scary? With your giant cobwebs and paper witch and jack-o'-lanterns?

i've made some realistic decomposing bodies of hanging child trick-or-treaters; three live black Dobermans tied with an old, nearly severed rope; and the stuffed corpse of my grandpa with dolls' eyes in a rocking chair on the porch with his pants off, one hand on his junk, the other holding a pistol pointed at you. All of this to circus music coming from inside.

Happy Halloween, motherfuckers.

"I just wanted to let you know that I've decided not to audition to narrate *Quickies*. I wish you the best, though."

—audiobook narrator

Does anyone know how to scratch the serial number off a gun?

"Christianity: the belief that some cosmic Jewish zombie can make you live forever if you symbolically eat his flesh and telepathically tell him you accept him as your master, so he can remove an evil force from your soul that is present in humanity because a rib-woman was convinced by a talking snake to eat from a magical tree."

"And what the overground media are doing is ensuring that we do not act on our responsibilities, and that the interests of power are served, not the needs of the suffering people, and not even the needs of the American people, who would be horrified if they realized the blood that's dripping from their hands because of the way they are allowing themselves to be deluded and manipulated by the system."

—Chomsky, 2002

"This is the type of man that empties the insane asylums. He doesn't propose a cure. He makes everybody crazy."

—Henry Miller, *Tropic of Capricorn*

Mosh pits always go counterclockwise.

"I would bury my dick so deep in that ass, whoever could pull it out would be crowned the next King Arthur."

—Gandhi

"An estimated 1 in 2,000 children born each year is neither boy nor girl. Germany is said to be the first European country to recognize this third gender, known as intersex."

—Charlie Angela, Al Jazeera

Hey, kids, wanna see a real scary Halloween house? This one is "upside down"—they owe more on it than it's worth. Now that's scary!

Is it more visual or a body high?
Wait for the drop.

> "I ate so much candy on Halloween, I'm worried about losing my foot today."
> —Arsenio Hall

This book will never be sold at an airport bookstore.

> "If you manage to bury people beneath loans they cannot repay and keep them entertained with sports, *American Idol*, and the sex lives of celebrities, you can control their desires and financial decisions. You can manipulate and exploit them."
> —John Perkins, *Hoodwinked* (2009)

> "If you manage to bury people beneath folds of genitalia and keep them entertained with prolapses, she-dicks, and the sex lives of amputees, you can control their desires and financial decisions. The Council can manipulate and exploit them."
> —Judy, Publicity

> "You are the average of the people you surround yourself with."
> —Sofia Coppola

"The point of public relations slogans like 'Support Our Troops' is that they don't mean anything. That's the whole point of good propaganda. You want to create a slogan that nobody is going to be against and I suppose everybody will be for, because nobody knows what it means, because it doesn't mean anything. But its crucial value is that it diverts your attention from a question that does mean something, do you support our policy? And that's the one you're not allowed to talk about."

—Noam Chomsky

"We watch shows about the rich and famous and in doing so, send messages to our children that they should aspire to living in mansions and traveling in private jets—regardless of how much environmental and social havoc is caused in the process."

—John Perkins, *Hoodwinked* (2009)

A 1985 profile of the Bravo TV channel in the *New York Times* observed that most of its programming consisted of international, classic, and independent films.

Bravo's lineup twenty-eight years later consists of *Shahs of Sunset*, *The Real Housewives of Atlanta*, *The Real Housewives of Beverly Hills*, *The Millionaire Matchmaker*, *The Real Housewives of Orange County*, *The Real Housewives of Miami*, *Top Chef*, and many more.

Is this what Bob Dylan meant when he said, "The times, they are a-changin'"?

That awkward moment when you realize you have been copying the writing style of a meme that doesn't even make a complete sentence.

"The world never permits a good-looking woman to starve."

—Henry Miller, *Tropic of Cancer*

i will write a sentence.

An amateur writer from the depths of hell, i will write a sentence.

An amateur writer from the depths of hell, i will write a sentence, attempting to trip you out and make you laugh.

An amateur writer from the depths of hell, i will write a sentence, attempting to trip you out and make you laugh, showing you that i can just keep adding these free modifiers to my base clause all day.

"They don't want you to vote. If they did, we wouldn't vote on a Tuesday. In November. You ever throw a party on a Tuesday? No. Because nobody would come."

—Chris Rock

"The jury is instructed to ignore common sense, logic, justice, and the 'big picture,' and consider only the minutiae and technical loopholes presented to you by these people who are paid to conceal the truth."

"I mean, they don't grade fathers. But if your daughter's a stripper, you fucked up."

—Chris Rock

"Bless me father for I will sin."

—Jack Kerouac

"The anus is gOD's loophole."

"Twenty percent of your customers provide 80 percent of your profit."

—Business 101

"Burner: wears goggles anytime, anywhere."

"Astrology: a convenient system to shift responsibility for people's fucked-up choices."

Ironic, isn't it, that Jesus was a hippie and Mohammad was a gypsy?

"Chakras out of alignment: I'm fucked up and looking for things to blame it on."

"Gifting: the act of dumping your useless crap on other people."

"Wiggas, jiggas, but i've been a Sand Digger all my life, and terrorists are profiled more than my brothas these days."

—DJ Ass Maggots

"Consumers can't report their drug dealers to the Better Business Bureau for selling them low-quality cocaine."

667, the NEIGHBOR of the Beast
i keep a real polo jockey on a baby grand piano in the back of my car. Fuck stereos.

"Manifest: how the enlightened mooch from their friends."

"America's ER doctors lead the globe in removing objects accidentally lodged in the rectum."
—Stephen Colbert

"You can get anything in this world if you generally don't want it."
—George Orwell

Women may have a G spot, but men have a P spot. *P* is for *prostate*.

If you're shopping on Thanksgiving, you're part of the problem.

"In the future, readers of newspapers and magazines will probably view news pictures more as illustrations than as reportage, since they will be well aware that they can no longer distinguish between a genuine image and one that has been manipulated."
—Andy Grundberg, "Ask It No Questions: The Camera Can Lie," the *New York Times*

One thing i miss about New York is the no-nonsense attitude of the NYPD. On one particular New Year's Eve, i had to pimp slap a dude who stole my taxi. He waved down a passing police car, but they bailed, laughing, after listening to him whine for twenty seconds. If it were LA, i would have been in jail for assault and battery.

"Science is a bit like the joke about the drunk who is looking under a lamppost for a key that he has lost on the other side of the street, because that's where the light is. It has no other choice."

—Noam Chomsky

"Knowledge is hot water on wool. It shrinks time and space."

—Mark Z. Danielewski, *House of Leaves*

"Universal love: what you feel when you're always high."

—the 2007 Guide to Deciphering Modern Hippie Star-Child Euphemistic Terminology

"The Council, the edgy secret Facebook group with the all-American good looks that became internationally famous with prolapsed rosebud anus porn, all died in a fiery car collision in Southern California. Their ages ranged from eighteen to sixty-five years old. The sad news was confirmed Saturday night by the Council's camp (because important people have 'camps') via their official Myspace account."

—Judy, Publicity Department

"Any sufficiently advanced technology is indistinguishable from magic."

—Arthur C. Clarke

"Managing a prostitute is like holding a tiger by the tail."

—Iceberg Slim

"I am against religion because it teaches us to be satisfied with not understanding the world."

—Richard Dawkins

"We are all atheists about most of the gods that humanity has ever believed in. Some of us just go one god further."

—Richard Dawkins, *The God Delusion*

"I have to think the people in Iraq will be in a better place [because of this war]. I have to believe that. Otherwise, this is just sheer madness."

—Major Martin Harnish, general surgeon

"The administrators of the Council are arguably the most unpleasant characters in all of nonfiction: jealous and proud of it; petty, unjust, unforgiving control freaks; vindictive, bloodthirsty ethnic cleansers; misogynistic, homophobic, racist, infanticidal, genocidal, filicidal, pestilential, megalomaniacal, sadomasochistic, capriciously malevolent bullies."

—Judy, Publicity (Richard Dawkins remix)

The Nazis were Christian.

"We should invade their countries, kill their leaders, and convert them to Christianity. We weren't punctilious about locating and punishing only Hitler and his top officers. We carpet-bombed German cities; we killed civilians. That's war. And this is war."
—Ann Coulter, *If Democrats Had Any Brains, They'd Be Republicans*

"Be thankful that you have a life, and forsake your vain and presumptuous desire for a second one."
—Richard Dawkins, interviewed by Gordy Slack in "The Atheist," Salon.com

"Only stone and steel accept my love."
—Morrissey, "I'm Throwing My Arms Around Paris"

"Now seriously, after all these hits and melodies, and memories you compare me to someone else! OMG! No offense to the other artists, but come on dawg, let's be honest, how many babies have been made off me?"
—R. Kelly

"Don't use the word 'gay' unless it's an acronym for 'Got Aids Yet.'"
—Bob Dornan, Rep. R-CA, American Taliban

"If you don't visit a bad neighborhood, it will visit you."

—Thomas L. Friedman

In only thirty years, the technology of "video" went from being a critical piece of evidence to being completely useless as evidence. In 1991, the televised beating of Rodney King by the LAPD showed the power of the all-seeing eye of video.

By the 2000s, directors were able to "doctor" film in such a way to make fiction look quite realistic, such as a basketball player making twenty half-court shots in a row or a lady getting hit by a car.

But by 2021, the ability to alter or completely generate false images by anyone with a computer made video useless as evidence. The landmark case in 2021 being that of four Long Beach police officers who had evidently been filmed trashing a church and having group sex with patients at a nursing home. They were acquitted of all charges, setting a new legal precedent of digitally manipulated technology and videos as a whole being non-admissible in court.

And just like that, we were back in the Dark Ages.

The Council: Numbers

LONG LIVE THE COUNCIL, PEACE UPON ITS PEN-GUINS AND SEALS. DEATH TO OUR ENEMIES. MAY THEIR BLOOD RUN IN THE STREETS. YE GODS. MAY THE COUNCIL GROW, FRUCTIFY, PROLAPSE, INGEST CONTRABAND, IMBUE 1989 L'YQUEM ONCE AGAIN, ETC.

> i just tried to donate two copies of my book. They said they have to send it to corporate for review. This will not end well.
>
> —at Hermosa Beach Public Library

If they don't accept it, i'll just stick one on the shelf.

> "To be fair, much of the Bible is not systematically evil but just plain weird, as you would expect of a chaotically cobbled-together anthology of disjointed documents, composed, revised, translated, distorted and 'improved' by hundreds of anonymous authors,

editors and copyists, unknown to us and mostly unknown to each other, spanning nine centuries."
—Richard Dawkins, *The God Delusion*

It is not an acceptable argument to say companies that use sweatshops in Bangladesh, Indonesia, China, and elsewhere are providing jobs. That's like saying slavery provided room and board.

The only *action* that businesses understand is the action of money. You can act by boycotting businesses that pay people three dollars a day to live in squalor, in dangerous work conditions, eighty hours a week, and in places that abuse women and children.

And don't say they can live like kings for three dollars a day until you go there and fucking try it.

If we're not fighting religious wars, how come all the graves at the military cemetery have crosses?

i'm still waiting to see a tombstone with the spaghetti-and-meatballs insignia.

Here comes Baphomet,
Here comes Baphomet,
Right down Anton Lane;
Ass Maggots and Slayer and all his foot soldiers,
Pullin' on the reins,
Ears are ringin',

Blasphemers singin',
All is scary all right.
Hang your selves and chant your spells,
'Cause Baphomet comes tonight!

"Does this upside-down cross make me look fat?"
"One glass of water will shut down midnight hunger pangs."

"In many states the highway patrol carries two gallons of Coca-Cola in the trunk to remove blood from the highway after a car accident."

"You can put a T-bone steak in a bowl of Coke and it will be gone in two days."

"The morning rush hour in LA is from 5:00 a.m. to noon. The evening rush hour is from noon to 7:00 p.m. Friday's rush hour starts on Thursday morning."

"LA has its own version of traffic rules: the car with the loudest muffler goes first at a four-way stop, followed by the truck with the biggest tires. However, SUV-driving, cell-phone-talking soccer moms *always* have the right of way."

"Never honk at anyone in LA. Ever. Seriously. It's an offense that can get you shot. If you actually stop at a yellow light, you will be rear-ended, cussed out, and possibly shot."

"Road construction is permanent and contiguous in all of LA and Orange Counties. Detour barrels are moved around for your entertainment pleasure during the middle of the night to make the next day's drive a bit more exciting."

"My time here is a mix of hustlers, vagrants, and dopers trying to steal my soul . . . one dirham at a time.

"They approach me asking for money in a series of currencies: 'Monsieur! Señor! Hey, YOU FUCKING JEW! Give me dirham. One euro. A DOLLAR!'

"I've decided to speak Russian to them because Russians are generally thought of as rude, violent, and short-tempered when traveling in Arab countries . . . or anywhere else, for that matter.

"'*NYET!*' I proclaim, but they are unfazed.

"After several attempts, between forty-three and fifty-seven, I stopped counting . . . the guy sat a few feet away and started huffing glue from a plastic bag.

"I promptly handed him ten euros and declared him 'council ambassador at large.'

"His name was Muhammad.

"He was my kind of scum!"
—Fabian at Grand Socco/Place du 9 Avril/Souk Barra, Morocco

The first step in getting old is saying you're getting old.

Din: a loud, confusing mixture of noises that lasts for a long time.

Usage: "The Council is a din of farts, queefs, vibrations, squeals, screams, hisses, pops, and bubbles."

"There was this twenty-five-year-old guy walking a tightrope across a deep river gorge while halfway around the world, another twenty-five-year-old guy was getting a blow job from a seventy-year-old-woman, but get this, at the exact same moment, both men were thinking the exact same thought. You know what it was? Don't look down."

—Mark Z. Danielewski,
House of Leaves

"It was important to say 'fuck' now and then, and say it loud too, relish its syllabic sweetness, its immigrant pride, a great American epic word really, starting at the lower lip, often the very front of the lower lip, before racing all the way to the back of the throat, where it finishes with a blast, the concussive of the *k* catching up then with the hush of the *f* already on its way, thus loading it with plenty of offense and edge and certainly ambiguity. FUCK."

—Mark Z. Danielewski,
House of Leaves

"How can you tell when a Burner gets lucky?"
"Two clean fingers."

"[S]he could reach up beneath me and press the tip of an oil soaked finger against my asshole, circling, rubbing, until finally she pushed hard enough to exceed the threshold of resistance, slipping inside me and knowing exactly where to go to, heading straight for the prostate, the P spot."

—Mark Z. Danielewski

Dear Muslim women:

Please liberate yourselves from the hair-covering hijabs and body-covering burqas forced upon you by your ruling male overlords.

Come to the West, where you can be as naked as we feel appropriate. Exploit yourself in new and degrading ways, including a bombardment of advertising laced in female flesh, or perhaps become a stripper and grovel around for dirty one-dollar bills.

We'll be waiting.

Lust,

Uncle Sam

"The Bechdel test asks whether a work of fiction features at least two women who talk to each other about something other than a man. Many contemporary works fail this test of gender bias."

"Bless your heart: ANTIQUATED southernism for 'fuck you,' often heard in open-plan offices where people are uncomfortable saying 'fuck you.'"

You cannot be persuaded. War is necessary and inevitable. i also cannot be persuaded. War is unnecessary and avoidable. If we agree to disagree, then you support the war effort financially, physically, and psychologically. i boycott it and just watch from the sidelines. You would prefer that because your war machine can continue without my participation. But i'm not OK with that. i must be involved. i either need to persuade you or i need to kill you. If i kill you, then i've already lost and am playing your game. So that only leaves one last question: Can you really not be persuaded?

"In a world full of pieces of shit, stick with the farters."
—Lung Butta
"I said that?"
—Lung Butta
"Yes."
—DJ Ass Maggots (this conversation was directed by Night Writer, Esq.)

"The first thing you need to know about Goldman Sachs is that it's everywhere. The world's most powerful investment bank is a great vampire squid wrapped around the face of humanity, relentlessly jamming its blood funnel into anything that smells like money."
—Matt Taibbi, *Griftopia: A Story of Bankers, Politicians, and the Most Audacious Power Grab in American History*

In feminist psychology, the terms *womb envy* and *vagina envy* denote the unexpressed anxiety that some men feel in natural envy of the biological functions of women (pregnancy, parturition, breast feeding)—emotions that impel their social subordination of women and drive them to succeed in perpetuating their names via material legacies.

Everybody wants to be a star. i want to be a fucking galaxy! And by that, i mean a black hole.

"Just sayin': shorthand for 'I have completed my bigoted statement.' See also: #sorrynotsorry."

This one goes out to all you old farts who post pictures of people in a room all on their cell phones, and you think that's the downfall of society because they're not talking to each other.

Would you approve if they were all reading newspapers or books? Guess what? i can read Homer's *Iliad*, send a message to my aunt in Denmark, and check the weather for my upcoming trip to Mexico, all while you sit there trying to make cliché small talk.

You probably also thought the wheel was the downfall of humanity because it destroyed long walks. i just realized you can't read this because you still have a flip phone with no internet access. Never mind (eBook joke).

If a female drinks beer at a bar, her personality is "casual, low maintenance, and down-to-earth."

The best way to approach her is to "challenge her to a game of pool."

"A room without books is like a body without a soul."

—Cicero

"Epic: lacking significance."
Usage: "That pizza was epic."

"You know you're getting fatter when your socks don't fit."

—Zach Galifianakis

"If a female orders mixed drinks at a bar (no umbrellas, such as a gin and tonic or scotch and soda), she is mature, has picky taste, and knows what she wants.

If she wants you, she'll send *you* a drink.

If a female orders water at a bar, she is pretentious and is looking for a serious relationship.

Don't approach her.

If a girl drinks wine at a bar, she is conservative, classy, and sophisticated.

Approach her by trying to weave Paris and clothing into the conversation.

If a man drinks water at a bar, he just threw up and is trying to wash the taste out of his mouth so that he can still get laid."

On Facebook:

> You're Blocked from Sending Friend Requests for 7 Days
>
> More people you've sent friend requests to have said they don't know you. To avoid being blocked in the future, please help us understand why you send friend requests.
>
> How are you using Facebook to connect with others?
>
> I would like to meet new people.
>
> I would like to follow celebrities and other high-profile people.
>
> I want to be friends with a lot of people.
>
> Other

"You are being shagged by a rare parrot."

What is "good"? What is "bad"? What is "good" to me might be considered "bad" or "kidnapping" by others.

I have the tattoo "John McEnroe Gland Slam 1984" on my gooch.

> "No true democracy is attainable when the process is determined by economic power."
>
> —Occupy Wall Street

I got an IED called FTP.

"The pinworm is the most common parasite in the United States. It lives in the gut. The female worm migrates to the human anus at night to deposit eggs. With poor hygiene the eggs are transmitted to the human mouth and swallowed. The hatched larvae migrate back into the intestine and restart the cycle."

You know you are working too hard when you are too tired to count your money.

"They have taken our houses through an illegal foreclosure process, despite not having the original mortgage."

—Occupy Wall Street

"On average, only two out of ten women are able to do proper Kegel exercises."

—AudioDigest Internal Medicine

"They have held students hostage with tens of thousands of dollars of debt on education, which is itself a human right."

—Occupy Wall Street

"They have continuously sought to strip employees of the right to negotiate for better pay and safer working conditions."

—Occupy Wall Street

"Now, if you'll excuse me, I have to go to the salon to dye my pubic hair white so my dick will look like Santa Claus."

—David Wong, *This Book Is Full of Spiders*

Missive (noun): a letter, esp. a long or official one.

Usage: "The boss hastily banged out massive electronic missives after banging his secretary out."

Synonyms: message, communication, letter, note, email, memorandum, line, communiqué, dispatch, news.

Sybarite: a person who is self-indulgent in their fondness for sensuous luxury.

Synonyms: hedonist, sensualist, voluptuary, libertine, pleasure-seeker, epicure, bon vivant, bon viveur.

Usage: "An exclusive resort that caters to DJ Ass Maggots and his cartel of wealthy sybarites."

William Ass Burroughs, Hunter Ass Thompson, DJ Ass Maggots.

It's a family tradition.

"A psychotic is a guy who's just found out what's going on."

—William S. Burroughs

Officer: Do you know how fast you were going?

Me: One hundred kilometers per hour. i believe that's 65 mph.

Officer: You a smart ass?
Me: No, sir. Just a fan of the metric system.

"Present-day irrealist writers cluster in what is called the Bizarro movement, a compendium of offbeat, underground, alternative writers who have banded together to promote their work. The Bizarro concept encompasses many different types of avant-garde writing, of which irrealism is one. Other genres, or sub-genres, represented under the Bizarro moniker are avant punk, new absurdism, subterficial fiction, dada street life, blender fiction, brutality chronic, tweeker lit, and dark hysteria."

"I don't fail. I succeed at finding what doesn't work."
—Christopher Titus

"When I grow up, I wanna be a doctor. A surgeon! A labia minora reconstructer and clitoroplasty reducer for female pseudohermaphrodites!"

"When you stop growing you start dying."
—William S. Burroughs, *Junkie*

"Perfectionism is the voice of the oppressor, the enemy of the people. It will keep you cramped and insane your whole life."
—Lamott

"It is evident that the two balls touched."
—Sir Isaac Newton

"I really wanted my shit to go viral, but HIV is not what I had in mind."

GREETINGS NEW MEMBERS!

As I sit here in my wheelchair, my decubitus-ulcered ass festering in feces, fapping to this midget (little person) with a strap-on, fucking a Goldman Sachs CEO up the poop chute, I brush my cape away from the keyboard to deliver this final message (until the next one) to all newbies:

CARRY ON THIS ORAL/ANAL/CYBER TRADITION FOR POSTERITY, as the OG Council members will all be dead soon. That is all.

Tapas: small plates without the small prices.

> "OK, dude, seriously. Enough. If you're scraping ancient internet memes for stuff to pass off as your own work, it's time to throw in the towel. Pro tip: if Steven Pinker has heard about it and put it in a book, it's probably too late for you to pretend to be the author."
>
> —Nathaniel Lee, managing editor of
> *Drabblecast*, after being
> overwhelmed by my s
> ubmissions from *Quickies!*

When a girl says she's "going back to dancing," what *you* think she means is she's "going back to stripping," but what she *really* means is she's "going back to whoring."

"Nice tan," she said.

"Thanks; it's jaundice."

You have to wait in so many lines at Coachella, it should be called Queuechella.

Forget about Pac versus Biggie. i'm still torn over the first rap feud: Hafez versus Rumi.

Just went from bad (gallstones) to worse (gallstone pancreatitis).

—at Mission Hospital

The hospital registration lady looked confused when i told her my religious affiliation is Church of the Flying Spaghetti Monster.

i can tell sports are important because all the commentators wear suits, and they spend so much time (money) on "in-depth" analysis and statistics.

i want someone who will accept me for who i'm not.

"Hello, sir, I would like to ask you some questions about your recent hospital stay. Please answer the next five questions about your race with a yes or a no. Do you consider yourself black?"

"Ummm. What?"

"A yes or a no, please."

"Well, technically no, i guess, but politically . . ."

"Do you consider yourself of Hispanic descent?"

"Viva La Raza."

"A yes or a no, please, sir."

"No."

"Do you consider yourself a Pacific Islander?"

"Does that include the Maldives?"

"I can't give any clarification, sir."

"No, then."

"Do you consider yourself Asian?"

"No."

"Do you consider yourself white?"

"Is this the last option? i'm Middle Eastern."

"This is the last question. Do you consider yourself white?"

"Is Middle Eastern white?"

"I can't give any clarification, sir."

"i don't know. i don't know if i'm white."

"We'll just put 'declined to answer.' Thank you, sir, and have a good evening."

World peace begins with nudity.

If you wish to send messages to the Council, please be advised we use only vintage late-1970s fax machines, a.k.a. telefax.

The meter maid asked me why I have a handicap placard on my Ferrari. i told her i have a broken heart. She gave me her phone number.

"Our lazy embrace of Jon Stewart and Stephen Colbert is a testament to our own impoverished comic standards. We have come to accept coy mockery as genuine subversion and snarky mimesis as originality. It would be more accurate to describe our golden age of political comedy as the peak output of a lucrative corporate plantation whose chief export is a cheap and powerful opiate for progressive angst and rage."

—Steve Almond, "The Joke's on You," the *Baffler*

"The Council, an international conglomerati of underground 'medicine' connoisseurs, sexual mavericks, music magnates, and financial barons, decentralized to locations ranging from Los Angeles to Chicago, Detroit, New York, Illinois, Miami, Cancun/Playa del Carmen, Dubai, Portland, Milan, Thailand, and the outernet."

—Judy, Publicity

nonplussed
adjective
1.
(of a person) surprised and confused so much that they are unsure how to react.
"I would be completely nonplussed and embarrassed at the idea of using 'nonplussed' in a sentence."

2.
North American

informal

(of a person) not disconcerted; unperturbed.

"Not giving a shit, I am nonplussed that 'nonplussed' can mean two different things—almost opposites, actually."

"Fake glasses are like blackface to nerds."

—Virgil Davis III

"Anarcho-syndicalism is a theory of anarchism that views revolutionary industrial unionism or syndicalism as a method for workers in capitalist society to gain control of an economy and, with that control, influence broader society. Syndicalists consider their economic theories a strategy for facilitating worker self-activity and as an alternative cooperative economic system with democratic values and production centered on meeting human needs.

"The basic principles of anarcho-syndicalism are solidarity, direct action (action undertaken without the intervention of third parties such as politicians, bureaucrats, and arbitrators), and direct democracy, or workers' self-management. The end goal of anarcho-syndicalism is to abolish the wage system, regarding it as wage slavery. Anarcho-syndicalist theory therefore generally focuses on the labor movement.

"Anarcho-syndicalists view the primary purpose of the state as being the defense of private property, and therefore of economic, social, and political privilege, denying most of its denizens the ability to enjoy material independence and the social autonomy that springs from it. In contrast with other bodies of thought, particularly with Marxism–Leninism, anarcho-syndicalists deny that there can be any kind of workers' state, or a state that acts in the interests of workers, as opposed to those of the powerful, and that any state with the intention of empowering the workers will inevitably work to empower itself or the existing elite at the expense of the workers. Reflecting the anarchist philosophy from which it draws its primary inspiration, anarcho-syndicalism holds to the idea that power corrupts."

Google has completely ruined my ability to bullshit people.

> "[A]nd it was leap year like now yes sixteen years ago my God after that long kiss I near lost my breath yes he said was a flower of the mountain yes so we are flowers all a woman's body yes that was one true thing he said in his life and the sun shines for you today yes that was why I liked him because I saw he understood or felt what a woman is and I knew I could always get round him and I gave him all the pleasure I could leading him on till he asked me to say yes and I wouldn't answer first only looked out over the sea and the sky I was thinking of so many things he didn't know of."
>
> —Molly Bloom (James Joyce's *Ulysses*)

> "My neighbors listen to good music, whether they like it or not."
>
> ". . . pink he wanted to touch mine with his for a moment but I wouldn't let him he was awfully put out

first for fear you never know consumption or leave me with a child embarazada that old servant Ines told me that one drop even if it got into you at all after I tried with the Banana but I was afraid it might break and get lost up in me somewhere because they once took something down out of a woman that was up there for years covered with lime salts they're all mad to get in there where they come out of you'd think they could never go far enough up and then they're done with you in a way till the next time yes because there's a wonderful feeling there so tender all the time how did we finish it off yes O yes I pulled him off into my handkerchief pretending not to be excited but I opened my legs I wouldn't let him touch me inside."

—Molly Bloom (James Joyce's *Ulysses*)

If you don't understand that you're running out of time, you haven't had enough near-death experiences.

There's always a louder muffler.

Jeers to Jon Stewart for giving former US Treasury Secretary Tim Geithner a nearly free ride and platform to sell his book last night on *The Daily Show*.

This former president of the Federal Reserve Bank of New York is one of the central figures in the subprime mortgage bailout and is another example of the duplicity of "our" government officials, who shack up with Wall Street. What a surprise—he now serves as president of Warburg Pincus, a Wall Street private equity firm.

Keep on letting these economic hitmen peddle their bullshit while my antibullshit sits on the shelves. Thanks, Jon Stewart.

This is not a recession, this is a great depression. This is global. And this is the one that we have had the privilege to see firsthand. We get to see the crawling insect underbelly of this "system."

Our financial leaders, with CDOs and credit default swaps, bet *against* the system! They made money because the subprime mortgage system failed, not in spite of it. What kind of lunatic system is this? How do you explain that to your kid?

Social media is changing the world. Facebook and Twitter have led to several Middle Eastern revolutions while also galvanizing American protests, such as Occupy Wall Street. Again, $5 billion has moved to credit unions during this movement.

This was about TV hosts propagating the lie. No, the revolution will not be televised, but it *will* be online.

THE END

Or is it?

www.ingramcontent.com/pod-product-compliance
Lightning Source LLC
Chambersburg PA
CBHW051946220626
47052CB00004B/811